William Glaister

Life of the Emperor Karl the Great

William Glaister

Life of the Emperor Karl the Great

ISBN/EAN: 9783337334079

Printed in Europe, USA, Canada, Australia, Japan

Cover: Foto ©Andreas Hilbeck / pixelio.de

More available books at **www.hansebooks.com**

KARL THE GREAT.

LIFE OF THE

EMPEROR KARL THE GREAT.

TRANSLATED FROM EGINHARD.

BY

WILLIAM GLAISTER, M.A., B.C.L.,

UNIVERSITY COLLEGE, OXFORD.

LONDON : GEORGE BELL & SONS, YORK STREET,
COVENT GARDEN.

1877.

LONDON:
PRINTED BY WILLIAM CLOWES AND SONS,
STAMFORD STREET AND CHARING CROSS.

PREFACE.

As the notes to this English edition of Eginhard's Life of Karl the Great are intended for the
use of young students of history, and profess only
to direct the attention briefly to what has been
insisted on at length by able historians, it may
be found useful to mention some of those English
writers in whose works the best information may
be obtained on this period of history. Gibbon's
"Roman Empire" is the standard work on the
history of the Empire, Greek and Latin, and of
the barbarian nations who invaded it.

On the Empire of Karl the Great and his
successors, the German Emperors of the Roman
Empire, their influence and pretensions, and on
the rise and power of the Papacy, Professor Bryce's
"Holy Roman Empire" is a work of interest
and repute. On the relations of the Gauls and the

Franks, Mr. Freeman's essay in his "Historical Essays." On the breaking up of the Karolingian Empire, and on the origin of modern France, vol. i. cap. iv. of Mr. Freeman's "Norman Conquest." For the character of the times, social and moral, as well as political, M. Guizot's "History of Civilization in France," and Hallam's "History of the Middle Ages." On the conquests of the Saracens in Spain and elsewhere, Mr. Freeman's "History of the Saracens" (1876). Also consult Spruner's "Historical Atlas," or the "Collegiate Atlas," which may be obtained at a less price.

There is an old history of Germany by a Mr. Savage (1702): it is rather a meagre book, but still it does set forth the lives and reigns of the Roman Emperors, from Karl the Great to Leopold the First, and contains an account of the ceremonies at the election and coronation of the Emperors.

Eginhard's "Life of Kaiser Karl" may be obtained in very simple and easy German, price 1*s.* 1*d.*

SOUTHWELL,
  1877.

CONTENTS.

KARL THE GREAT.

CHAPTER I

ON EGINHARD.

EGINHARD was by birth a German, an Austrasian Frank, born towards the close of the reign of King Pippin the Short. He was taken into the service of King Karl when very young, and was brought up at the school attached to the palace at Aachen, under the eye of the learned Alcuin. While there he was on terms of the greatest intimacy and friendship with the children of the King. On his reaching manhood, Karl made him his secretary and private chaplain, and from that time he became the Emperor's most constant counsellor and companion, never leaving his side in peace or war, except on the single occasion when he took his will to Rome to receive the signature of the Pope.

B

Eginhard was also superintendent of the Emperor's works, such as the palace which he caused to be built at Ingelheim and the bridge over the Rhine at Mainz.

Karl presented him to the Abbey of S. Bavon in Ghent, and after Karl's death the Emperor Ludwig gave him the domain of Seligenstadt, where he built an abbey, to which he retired soon after the death of Karl, and there died and was buried in 844.

Raban Maur, Archbishop of Mainz, and Eginhard's contemporary, wrote his epitaph, describing him as—Vir nobilis, ingenio prudens, probus actu, ore facundus.

Though Eginhard's Life of Karl, written in Latin, a language in which he confesses he was little versed, is so short as not to fill more than forty ordinary pages, it was, nevertheless, the greatest literary production of that age. "It was," remarks M. Guizot, "the most distinguished piece of history from the sixth to the eighth century ; indeed, the only one which can be called a history. For it is not a mere chronicle, but a real political biography, written by one who was an eye-witness of the events he narrates, and who understood their importance."

It was the first attempt at history writing since the great works of antiquity, and that, too, by a barbarian.

The work is characterized throughout by the greatest simplicity and apparent thoughtfulness, and by freedom from all extravagance and exaggeration. It is a thoroughly trustworthy narrative of the life of the great Karl, and it is noteworthy that from first to last it contains no groundwork for the romances of a later date.

Gratitude for the Emperor's friendship, and admiration for his character and work, prompted Eginhard to undertake the office of his historian, and well and faithfully has he performed it. His history has always been, and must ever remain, the one great authority for the reign of the Emperor Karl the Great.

The other works of Eginhard that have come down to us, some letters, and his annals of the years 741–829, do not bear the same high literary character.

DESCENT OF HILDERIC III., LAST OF THE MERWINGS.

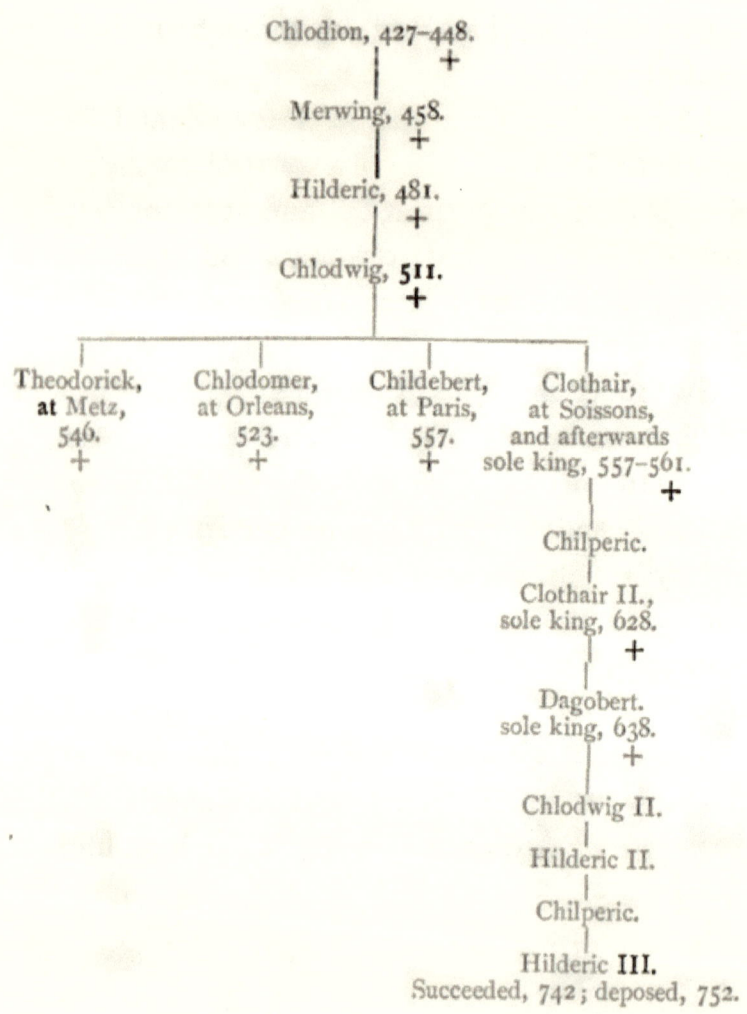

Chlodion, 427–448.
✢

Merwing, 458.
✢

Hilderic, 481.
✢

Chlodwig, **511.**
✢

| Theodorick, **at** Metz, 546. ✢ | Chlodomer, at Orleans, 523. ✢ | Childebert, at Paris, 557. ✢ | Clothair, at Soissons, and afterwards sole king, 557–561. ✢ |

Chilperic.

Clothair II., sole king, 628. ✢

Dagobert. sole king, 638. ✢

Chlodwig II.

Hilderic II.

Chilperic.

Hilderic **III.**
Succeeded, 742; deposed, 752.

THE KARLINGS

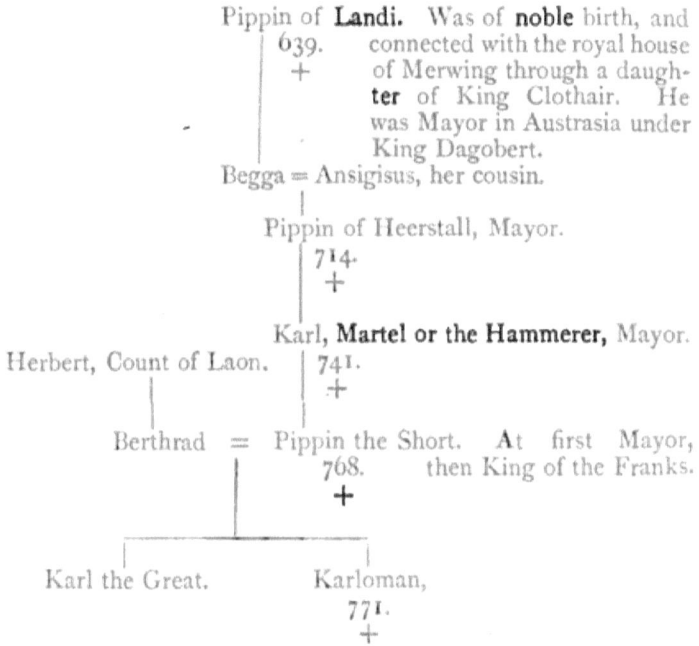

Pippin of **Landi.** Was of **noble** birth, and
639.   connected with the royal house
+   of Merwing through a daughter of King Clothair. He
was Mayor in Austrasia under
King Dagobert.

Begga = Ansigisus, her cousin.

Pippin of Heerstall, Mayor.
714.
+

Karl, **Martel or the Hammerer,** Mayor.

Herbert, Count of Laon.   741.
+

Berthrad   =   Pippin the Short.   At first Mayor,
768.   then King of the Franks.
+

Karl the Great.   Karloman,
771.
+

CHAPTER II.

ON THE FRANKS.

THE Franks (*frech*, fierce or bold) were **a** tribe **or** tribes of Teutons speaking the old Low German tongue. They **are** not known to history until the middle of the third century, when their hostile encroachment brought them into collision with the Roman Empire. Their earliest settlements were between the rivers Scheld and Rhine. In the third and fourth centuries we read of them as being the **enemies** of the Romans, at whose expense they greatly enlarged their territories along the banks of the Rhine and in the north of Gaul. **The** old Roman cities of **Mainz, Trier, and** Köln more than once experienced their fierce and desolating attack, and **at** last became permanent **Frankish** possessions and **Köln** their **chief town.**

In the fifth century, under Chlodion, the first
Frankish King identified in history, they
extended their southern boundary as far
A.D.
427–448.
as the river Somme; and though, on this
encroachment, the Roman general, Ætius, engaged
and defeated them, they succeeded in **retaining**
possession of the country they had occupied.

For some years from this time they laid aside
their hostility to the Romans, and were regarded
rather as the allies of the Empire, and its bulwark
against other northern barbarian invaders. In the
great battle of Chalons-sur-Marne they
ranged themselves, as did the Visigoths,
451.
under the standard of Ætius, and aided the
Romans in delivering Europe from the scourge of
Attila and his Huns. Merwing was then their King.

There were two great divisions or tribes of
the Franks—the Salians, deriving their name probably from the river Isala, the Yssel, who dwelt
on the Lower Rhine, **and** the Ripuarians, probably
from *Ripa*, **a bank,** who dwelt about the banks of
the Middle **Rhine.** **The** latter were by far the
most numerous, **and** spread over a greater extent
of country ; but **to** the Salians belongs the glory of
founding **the** great Frankish Kingdom under the
royal line **of** the Merwings.

Each tribe had **its** own independent King and government, and separate territories, until **the acces-sion** of King Chlodwig, who succeeded to the throne **of the** Salian Franks **by in-**heritance, **and** was afterwards chosen **by** the Ripu-arians as their King also.

481.

In this union **of** Frankish tribes **under** Chlodwig, ⌡ we notice **the** first great German **or** Teutonic[1] confederation. The Franks, **at** this **time** heathen worshippers **of** the old Teuton gods, Thor and Woden, were a tall, light-haired, blue-eyed people ; **fierce** warriors, often cruel and savage in their war-fare, but more amenable to constituted govern-ment, of more settled habits, less wayward and passionate, and **of** nobler instincts **and** aspira-tions, than **any** other **barbarian** invaders **of** the Empire. This great difference must be well marked, that whereas **the** invasions of the Goths, Vandals, Lombards, Burgundians, and others had been **the** transportation and migration **of** the whole tribe or **nation** from their original settlements towards warmer districts and richer countries, towards the wealth of the great cities of the Empire, **and, above**

---

[1] The word **Teuton** is from **Theod,** *the people,* as opposed to Welsh, *foreigners.* Deutschen, **as** the Germans **call** themselves, is the same word : **so** also Dutch.

all, to the one great centre of attraction, of civilization and luxury, Rome,—it was the object and aim
of the Franks to build up their own Kingdom in
their own German Fatherland, and to enhance its
glory and secure its power and permanence by
enlarging its borders around its original centre on
the banks of the Rhine.

The great conquests of the Franks were made
under Chlodwig, who succeeded to the leadership
of their united tribes at the early age of eighteen.
A war-band of probably not more than six thousand warriors followed his standard, the bulk of the
nation remaining in their own homes and settlements.

Chlodwig's first notable victory was won at
Soissons, over Syagrius, who ruled over what
remained of Roman dominion in the north of
Gaul.[1] This victory gave the Franks all Gaul as
far as the river Loire, which immediately
received a wave of Teuton settlers, who
occupied the country like a colonizing militia. 486.

His second great victory was over kindred

---

[1] It must be borne in mind that the country between the Rhine
and the Pyrenees can be distinguished at this time, and for many
centuries after, by no other name than "Gaul," whether under
the rule of Visigoth or Frank.

Teutons, the Alemanni—*all-men's league*—who dwelt on the Upper Rhine, and who seem at **this** time to have formed a South German confederation, and to be contending with the Franks for German ascendency.[1] Chlodwig entirely broke the South German power in the battle of Zülpich, and **496.** compelled the tribes of the Alemanni league **to come** into the Frankish confederation, thereby extending the Frankish dominion over South Germany as far **as** the river Inn and the range **of the** Alps.

After this victory Chlodwig embraced Christianity. In **the** heat of the hard-fought and long-doubtful battle, **he had** invoked the aid **of** the God of the Christians **and of his** Burgundian bride Chlotild, and, in humble **gratitude** for the victory, he **and his** chieftains and army of warriors received **the sacrament** of baptism **at the** hands of Remigius, **the Bishop of** Rheims. From that time the Franks became **the** most devoted servants of their new faith, **and** the willing and foremost champions of the Church of Christ. Chlodwig's arms were **soon** employed in her **cause.**

---

[1] Compare the North **and** South German—the Prussian and Austrian—war of 1866, **which** was for the same object ; and the battle of Königgrätz led to precisely the same results.

His third **great victory was over** the Visigoths,[1]
whose realm then . extended over all Spain, and
Gaul as far as the river Loire **and the** confines
of the Burgundians.[2] Chlodwig's avowed motive **for**
this **war** was to **win** for the Catholics the fairest
portion of Gaul, **which** he grieved **that the Aryan**
Visigoths should still possess. The **Goths**
were defeated **on** the plains of Poictiers, **507.**
that frequent battle-field, and were compelled **to**
relinquish their Gallic possessions.

Thus **all** the country **from the Loire** to the
Pyrenees was added to **the** Frankish dominion.[3]
The Burgundians **also were** brought into sub-
jection.

The reign of Chlodwig was greatly distinguished
by these brilliant successes of the Frankish arms.
The Franks came **now to be regarded as** the rising
power in Europe, **and** the possible regenerators of

[1] The Visigoths had established themselves **in Spain** and
Aquitain about one hundred years **before the Frankish** conquest.
Two hundred years **later** (711) **they** lost Spain **to the** Moors, and
their name disappears from history.

[2] The Burgundians had established their kingdom on the Rhone
in 406.   It was destroyed **by** the sons of Chlodwig.

[3] **With** the exception of Septimania, a narrow strip along the
coast **of the** Mediterranean, between the Pyrenees **and** the river
Rhone, which the Goths retained for some years longer.

political society from that chaos into which it had everywhere fallen.

The Emperor Anastatius confirmed Chlodwig in his conquests, and brought him into connexion with the Empire by conferring upon him the Roman dignity of Consul. Barbarian chiefs, who had won a possession within the limits of the Empire, were much gratified by being invested with such empty titles. The investiture was value-less. It serves only to show the power which the Roman name exercised over barbarian minds, and the abject weakness of the Emperors in thus decorating the invaders and destroyers of the Empire.

On the death of Chlodwig, his Kingdom was divided among his four sons. Their re-spective seats of government were at Metz, Orleans, Paris, and Soissons. Clothair, the youngest, survived to reign over the whole, but it was again divided at his death. The entire realm was afterwards united again, under Clothair II. and his son Dagobert. It was then again divided. Some of Chlodwig's descend-ants also became Kings in Aquitain, and others in Burgundy. But the many different partitions which occurred at different dates all gave way to the two

511.

**613-628
-638.**

great divisions or kingdoms of the Austrasian [1]
or Eastern Franks, who were the pure German
Franks of the old home country about the Rhine,
having Metz and Köln for their chief towns; and
the Neustrian or Western Franks, who were settlers
in the conquered part of North Gaul. These latter
were rapidly losing their purity of blood and speech,
by intermingling with the more numerous Romano-
Celtic population among whom they dwelt.

The Neustrians took for their chief town Soissons, and afterwards Laon.

The descendants of Merwing reigned on both
thrones. History tell us of no weaker or more
worthless line of Kings than these Merwings. They
are known as the "Insensati," or Do-Nothing-Kings.
The power which had been so vigorously wielded
by Chlodwig slipped from their feeble grasp into
the hands of their chief officer of state, the Mayor
of the palace. As the incapacity of the Merwings
obliged this officer to discharge the duties of the
King, so it enabled him to usurp the power.
This he was not slow to do. Another element

---

[1] Austrasian, *Oester-reich*, the Eastern Kingdom; so Austria, the
Eastern March; Neustrian, *Ne-oester-reich*, that is, the Western
Kingdom.

contributing to the power of the Mayor was the growth in importance of the German or Austrasian aristocracy—the great nobility, who were not unwilling to see the power of the Crown curtailed, and many of its privileges discharged by one of their own order. The Mayor, from being a servant of the King about the palace, grew into the representative and leader of an aristocracy which had now become an hereditary nobility.

The natural loyalty of the Frankish people to an old-established royal family caused the Mayors of the palace to proceed with the greatest caution in their design of supplanting the house of Merwing.

The family of Pippin of Landi filled the office of Mayor in Austrasia for several generations; in fact, the office had become hereditary. The long-tried valour and ability of that family, in the field and in the council chamber, had well commended it to those Frankish nobles who had the greatness and glory of the Kingdom at heart.

Although, at the last moment, Pippin the Short thought it better and safer to obtain the sanction of an altogether new and foreign authority—the Pope—before he transferred the crown of Hilderic III. to his own head, the revolution was effected without a voice being raised or a blow struck in favour of the degenerate descendant of the mighty Chlodwig.

During the Mayorship **of** Pippin **of Heerstall** (though **this** was more than half a century before the final removal of the Merwings, **680-714.** it is easier to date by the **Mayor** than by the **King**) there was much fighting between the Austrasians and the Neustrians—not, indeed, for the first time; but now **a war occurred of a** far more momentous and **decisive character.**

Such a war cannot be called a civil war **in** the **Frankish** nation. **In the** two **hundred** years that **had** elapsed since **the** colonization **of North** Gaul by **the Franks, the** Frankish settlers had been entirely lost among the **old Celtic population. The** Gallo-Roman element **had now quite absorbed the** Teutonic. **It** was a war, **therefore, of pure Teutons** —Austrasian Franks—Germans **in blood and in** speech, **against Gallo-Celts, speaking the Romano-Gallic** *patois,* **the** *Romana rustica,* **for such had the** Neustrians **now become.**

The success which **attended the arms of** Pippin **and** the Austrasian **aristocracy in this war,** **687.** **on the field** of Testry, must **be considered**

as a great German national **victory. It brought
about the** complete overthrow **of the** Neustrian
power, **was a** death-blow **to the line** of the Merwings, **and** delayed for **two hundred** years the
formation of an independent Kingdom in the north
of Gaul.[1]

By the victory of Testry, Neustria **seemed to
be a second** time conquered **by the German**
Franks. Pippin assumed **the** government of **the**
Neustrians **as** their Mayor, **as well as of the**
Austrasians, and all **the territories of** the Frankish
confederation were again united under the sceptre
of one superior Lord.

It **was** in this state and under these circumstances that they were **handed** down to **Pippin's**
great-grandson, Karl the Great.

---

[1] That is, until the division of the Empire on the **death** of Karl
the Fat (888), when another Kingdom of Neustrian or Western
Franks was **attempted,** ruled **over by** Karling princes, with their
seat of government **at Laon.** This Kingdom only lasted a hundred
years, and during **that** time there **was** always **the** possibility of its
reverting **to the Empire,** and again merging with the Eastern
Franks, as **after Testry.** But **on the death** of the last of the line of
German Kings **at** Laon (987), the people of North Gaul exercised the
right of electing a King of their **own** Celtic nationality and their
own Romano-Gallic speech. **Their choice** fell on Hugh, the Duke
of Paris. Thus the Kingdom of Paris, or modern France, dates from
the end of the tenth century, and Hugh is the first French King.

CHAPTER III.

'ON KARL.

KARL, called "The Great," King of the Franks 768–
814, and Roman Emperor 800–814, was German
born, though the exact place of his birth is uncertain ; he spoke the German language, the old Low
German tongue, wore the German dress, and made
his home in the old German town of Aachen, or at
his palace at Ingelheim near Mainz, or at Nymeguen on the Waal. He was thoroughly German
in all his habits and manners of private life, but
his public government was conducted on Roman
principles, and his realm administered according
to the traditions of the old Roman Empire. He
was a barbarian [1] who had adopted Roman ideas

---

[1] Barbarian—this term was first used by the Greeks to denote
those who did not live in Hellas, and who did not speak Greek.
They afterwards applied it to those who did not speak Greek cor-

C

and Roman principles of statesmanship. We need not think Karl singular in this union of Roman thought with German life. Other barbarians had before attempted the same thing. Nor was it at variance with the theories and notions of those over whom he ruled. Weak as the Roman power had for some time been, the best traditions connected with the Roman name and Imperial government had been handed down from its strongest days, and taken deep root in the minds of those barbarians who had broken into the Roman provinces, and who had settled among people still governed by Roman laws and speaking the Roman tongue.

The barbarians, while they despised and trampled upon the degenerate descendants of the great Cæsars and Roman people, could not but admire that system of government which had made itself feared in all the world, and under which, they saw, men grew up law-abiding, rich, prosperous, and luxurious, living in fine cities adorned with magnificent buildings full of treasures and works of

rectly, *ore rotundo molliter ac Atticè.* It was afterwards applied by the Romans to all who did not speak Greek or Latin. It is used in the same sense in the Bible, Rom. i. 14 and 1 Cor. xiv. 11. "*Barbarus hic ego sum quia non intelligor ulli.*"—Ovid. "*Ungrieche*" in German.

art.   **They** would turn **out** the present unworthy inheritors **of a** great **name and principle, and play** the Roman themselves.

The Roman Empire, **by past** traditions **and** present belief, was to the barbarians **the** symbol of law and order ; **and to** the better thinking among them, and **to the** older population, it seemed to **be** the **right** state **of** things, fitting and necessary **to** the world's well-being. They **saw** in the Empire one central **and universal** authority—order and unity, as **opposed** to **barbarian** disorganization and chaos. **Karl** was himself **a grand** embodiment of these feelings, and **his** reign an enduring revival of these principles.

The **theory of the** Roman Empire still continued **to** exercise **a** strong influence over men's minds long **after** actual facts plainly pointed **out its** failure.

The question of the **right of** the Roman citizens to elect, and the Pope **to crown** and consecrate, the Roman **Emperor,** cannot **be** entered **upon** here. It need only **be said that the nations of the** west of Europe **regarded** Karl **as** the rightful successor, in law and in fact, **not only of the old Roman** Cæsars, but of the Constantinopolitan Emperors as **well, and** hailed with delight **the recovery** by Rome of her ancient prerogative of electing the **Emperors** of the Roman Empire.

From the **time** of **Karl the** Great, whoever **was** chosen by the German people **to be** their King became thereby "Emperor elect;" and when he had been crowned by **the** Pope, amid the acclamation of the Romans, his full title of Roman Emperor was complete, and he acquired the subject Kingdom of Italy, **with** such rights **and** powers **as he** might **be able to** enforce.

Meantime, the right **of the** whole German people **to elect** their King, **and the** "Emperor elect," came to be exercised **by a small** college of the great German nobility, its members being called the Seven **Electors.** They **were** the Archbishops of the three great dioceses, Mainz, Trier, **and Köln,** and the representatives of **the** four great German nations—the Count Palatine of the **Rhine, for** the Franconians; the Margrave of Brandenburg, for the Swabians; the Duke of Saxony, for **the** Saxons; and the King of Bohemia, for the Bavarians. The election was **at** Frankfort. The coronation as King **of the** Germans was at Aachen, as King of Burgundy at Arles, **as King** of Italy at Milan, as Emperor of the Roman Empire **by** the Pope at Rome.

It was thus that the Roman Empire was còn-
stituted during the Middle Ages ; and the election of the German King to be the Roman Emperor,
which was begun in the person of Karl the Great,
was continued until the abdication of Francis II.
in 1806, when the last successor of Augustus resigned the Imperial crown, and the Roman Empire
came to an end.

ROMAN EMPIRE, PAPACY, AND CONTEMPORARY POWERS.

ROMAN EMPERORS.	POPES.	ENGLAND.	CALIPHS OF BAGDAD.	KING OF GALLICIA AND ASTURIAS.
A.D.	A.D.	A.D.	A.D.	A.D.
775. Leo IV.	768. Stephen.	757-796. Offa, King of the March-land.	776-786. Al-Modi.	
780-797. Constantine VI.	772. Adrian I.			791-843. Alfonso II. el Casto.
	795. Leo III.			
800. Karl the Great.		802-836. Egbert, King of West Saxons, and Lord of England.	786-809. Haroun-al-Raschid.	
In the East.			809-813. Al-Mamoun.	
802. Nicephorus.				
811. Michael I.				
813. Leo V.				
	816. Stephen IV.			
814. Ludwig I.				
840. Lothar I.				

CHAPTER IV.

EGINHARD'S **LIFE OF THE** *EMPEROR* **KARL THE GREAT.**

PREFACE.

WHEN I had made up my mind to describe the public and private life, and to some considerable extent the exploits, of my master who nurtured me, Karl, the most noble and justly famous King, I comprised the subject within the smallest compass within my power ; taking care not to neglect what might come to my knowledge thereon, and also not to offend, by a too lengthy narration of each new particular, the taste of the most fastidious, if indeed it can in any way be avoided that they are not offended by modern-day writings, who view with disdain the chronicles of ancient date compiled by the most learned and accomplished men.

And although I cannot doubt there are very

many, possessed of leisure and addicted to letters, who consider that the state of the present age ought not to be so neglected, that everything which is now taking place should pass into silence and oblivion, as though it were unworthy of any remembrance, and, seduced by the desire of posthumous fame, wish to record the noble deeds of others in any description of writing, rather than they should, by writing nothing, withhold the fame of their own name from the cognizance of posterity ; still, I did not think that I ought to restrain myself from composition even of this kind, since I was conscious that no one could describe more accurately than I could matters in which I was myself concerned, and which, eyewitnessed, as they say, I faithfully took note of at the time, and whether they would be recorded by another hand I could not clearly know.

I therefore judged it better to hand down to posterity the same records, as it were in common with other writings, rather than that the brilliant life of the noblest King, the greatest of all in his age, and that actions the most distinguished, and by men of modern times little likely to be imitated, should be allowed by me to perish in the shades of oblivion.

There was in the background **yet another** cause, **and** one, in my opinion, not unreasonable, which, standing by itself, might **even be** sufficient to induce **me** to write this history, viz., **the nurture** bestowed upon me and the friendship with himself and his children, which, from the time when **I first** began to frequent his palace, **was never inter-** rupted ; by these ties he so bound me and made me his debtor in life and death that I **should with** justice seem **to be, and be** judged **to be, most** ungrateful **if,** unmindful **of so many** kindnesses bestowed upon me, **I** were to **pass** over in silence the brilliant deeds of **one** who deserved so well of me, and were **to allow his** life, as though he had never **lived,** to remain without a written remem- brance and the praise which is its due.

But to describe and **duly** to unfold this subject, **not my** small talent, meagre **and poor as it is—** nay, rather **I** had **said which** hardly **exists at all** —but **the** unflagging **rhetoric of a Tully had** sufficed.

Here, however, reader, **is** the **book which** con- tains the memorial **of this** great and most famous man, **in which** there **is** nothing, **save only his** noble deeds, to wonder at, unless haply you wonder that **I, a** barbarian, **too little** versed **in the Roman**

tongue, should have thought that I could write
with any degree of elegance or propriety in Latin,
and should so far have transgressed the bounds of
modesty as to imagine that I might despise the
saying of Cicero, who, speaking of the Roman
historians, as we read in the first book of his
" Tusculans," says, " For any one to commit his
thoughts to writing, who can neither arrange nor
illustrate his ideas, nor by any pleasing art attract
the reader, is the work of a man who recklessly
misuses both leisure and books."

This dictum of the consummate orator had,
indeed, deterred me from writing, only that I held
a preconceived opinion that it would be better for
me by writing to experience the criticism of men,
and make venture of my own small ability, rather
than by sparing myself to pass over the memory
of so great a man.

THE LIFE OF KARL.

THE Franks in olden times used to choose their
Kings from the family of the Merwings, which royal
line is considered to have come to an end
in the person of Hilderic III., who was
deposed from the throne by command of Stephen,

A.D.
752.

the Roman **Pontiff, when his long hair was cut off** and he was placed **in a** monastery.[1]

Although the **line of the** Merwings actually ended **with** Hilderic, **it had** nevertheless for some time previously been **so** utterly wanting in power that **it had** been **able to show** no mark of royalty except **the** empty **kingly** title. **All the resources** and power of the Kingdom had **passed into the** hands of the Prefects of the **palace, who were called the " Mayors of the palace," and by** them the supreme government was administered. Nothing was left to the **King. He had to content** himself **with** his royal **title, long hair, and** hanging beard.[2] **Seated in a** chair **of state,** he used to display an appearance of power by receiving foreign ambassadors on their arrival, **and by giving** them **on** their departure, as if on **his own** authority, those answers **which he had been** taught or com- **manded to** give.

Thus, except **his useless title, and an** uncertain allowance **for his subsistence, which the** Prefect **of**

[1] The process of deposition **took** place at the **annual** assembly of the people **at Soissons,** in March, 752, when Pippin **was** proclaimed King, **and** was consecrated by S. Boniface, Archbishop of Mainz.

[2] The **long hair,** hanging **down** the back **and shoulders, was** the distinctive mark of royalty **among the Franks ; the rest of the** nation were obliged **to cut their hair** short.

the palace used to furnish at his pleasure, there
was nothing that the King could call his own,
unless it were the profits of a single farm, and that
a very small one, where was his home, and where
he had such servants as were needful to wait on
him, and who paid him the scanty deference of
a most meagre court.

Whenever he went anywhere he used to travel in
a waggon drawn by a yoke of oxen, with a rustic
oxherd for charioteer. In this manner he pro-
ceeded to the palace, and to the public assemblies
of the people held every year for the despatch of
the business of the Kingdom,[1] and he returned
home again in the same sort of state. The administration of the Kingdom, and every matter which
had to be undertaken and carried through, at home
and abroad, was managed by the Mayor of the
palace.[2]

[1] These were the primitive popular assemblies of the Franks,
the Placita or Plaids, held every year in the month of March, in the
open air ; hence the March-field, the Champ de Mars. They were
legislative assemblies, and all the business of the Kingdom was then
transacted. They had fallen into disuse en the growing up of the
aristocratic power of the great nobles under the later Merwings.
Pippin of Heerstall is thought to have revived them, the time of
holding them being changed from March to May. They were
afterwards entirely superseded by the Diet, or council of great
nobles.

[2] The Mayor was at first merely one of the household appointed

2. At the time of the deposition of Hilderic the office of Mayor was filled by Pippin, the father of King Karl. The office seemed now to be almost hereditary; for Pippin's father, Karl,[1] had also held it, and with great renown, since he had quelled throughout all Frank-land those usurpers who had tried to assume independent authority.[2] He had also utterly defeated the Saracens, who were at that time attempting to establish themselves in Gaul, in two great battles, the first in Aquitain, near the city of Poictiers, and the second near Narbonne on the river Birra, and had compelled them to retire into Spain.[3]

by the King. He afterwards became the chief of the King's great vassals, or "Antrustions," as they were called—"those in the King's trust"—who in time began to interfere in his election. The Mayor then became the head of the nobility rather than the servant of the crown. The Frankish court soon became very aristocratic, and began to assume much state and ceremony; under the Mayor were the Seneschal, Marshal, Chancellor, Chamberlain, Constable, Sewer —offices all filled by great nobles; then came the Dukes, Counts, and lesser nobility.

[1] Karl was an illegitimate son, and his father would have disinherited him, but he escaped from his prison and was acknowledged by the Austrasian nobles. There were some attempts to throw off his authority.

[2] The Neustrians endeavoured to set up a Mayor of their own; the Duke of Toulouse revolted; the Aquitanians rebelled; the Frisians also.

[3] After the defeat inflicted by Chlodwig (507), the Visigothic

Karl **had** himself also **been** preceded **in** the
Mayorship by his father, Pippin, **an** honour which

monarchy had been transferred from Toulouse to Toledo. On the
invasion of the Moors of Africa (711), the Goths lost to them in one
battle all Spain, with the exception of some strongholds in the
mountains of Asturias, where **the** Spanish nobles revived the
Christian monarchy under Don Pelayo, at Oviedo, **and** growing and
gaining, they **won** back, bit **by bit,** in seven hundred years of constant war, all that had been **lost to the** Mahometans in a single
battle. The Saracens, not **content** with the conquest **of** Spain, had
invaded Gaul (in 721 and **725), and** had committed great ravages in
Burgundy. They were now advancing with an enormous host, bent
on **conquering the** Frankish Kingdom. **No battle** on which such
momentous **issues** hung **had been fought in** Europe since Chalons
(451). It was then the **Tatar Hun who** threatened Europeans with
destruction; now **the Mahometan Moors** seemed about to over-
whelm Christendom. **The** fate of Europe rested on the generalship
of Karl and the valour **of** his Franks. Chalons had been won by
the foot soldiers, the **last effort** of the Roman legions; Poictiers was
a cavalry battle, where the weighty German horse received, unshaken,
the headlong charges **of** Moorish chivalry. At last the Moors were
taken in **the** rear, and **a** charge of the Franks put them to flight.
The slaughter **of the** infidels was immense, and the spoils of a
luxurious camp enriched the victors. The thanks **of** Europe were
due to Karl, **who** acquired **by** his prowess the name of the
" Hammerer."

All the great battles of Europe, from about this time until the
middle **of** the fourteenth century, were essentially cavalry battles.
The horse—the heavy-armoured knights, German or Norman ; the
clouds of Hungarian, Moorish, and Polish chivalry, were irresistible
by footmen. It was not until the time of Crecy that the accuracy
of the English bowmen, and, in the struggle with Austria, the firmness of the Swiss pikemen, restored the balance between horse and
foot.

was conferred by the people only on those who
were distinguished from the commonalty by their
noble birth and great wealth.

When Pippin had held for some years this office
(nominally as the lieutenant of King Hilderic)
which had descended from father and grandfather
to himself and his brother Karloman, and had
been by them jointly administered with the
greatest goodwill, Karloman, we know not why,
but probably because he desired a more
secluded life, relinquished the arduous
government of a temporal Kingdom and betook
himself to a private life at Rome. While he
was there he became a monk, and put on the
dress of the order. Having built a monastery
on Mount Soracte, adjoining the Church of
S. Sylvester, he there enjoyed for several years
the repose he sought for, in company with the
brothers of the order who had gone with him.
He was, however, obliged to change his place
of residence, because many of the Frankish
nobility, when making pilgrimages to Rome to
fulfil their vows, broke, by their frequent visits to
him, that quiet which he most of all desired, since
they were unwilling to pass by unnoticed one
who had formerly been their King. As constant

747.

interruptions of this sort hindered the object of his retirement, he withdrew to the Monastery of S. Benedict[1] on Mount Casino, in the province of Samnium, and there passed the remainder of his life in religious exercises.

3. Pippin, however, who by the authority[2] of the Roman Pontiff, from being the Mayor of the palace, had risen to be the King, governed the Franks solely in his own person for fully fifteen years. He died of dropsy at Paris towards the close of the Aquitanian war, which he had begun against Waifar, the Duke of that country, and which was carried on continuously during nine years. He left two sons, Karl and Karloman, who by God's will succeeded to the Kingdom.

768.

The Franks, in a general assembly convened with much solemnity, appointed them both Kings, as soon as they had agreed to the following conditions :—For the purposes of government the whole realm was to be equally divided ; Karl was

---

[1] S. Benedict, the reformer of the western monks. He built the monastery on Mount Casino (528). Almost all the most distinguished men, statesmen, scholars, and churchmen, between the seventh and twelfth centuries, were of the Benedictine order.

[2] The word used here is " *Auctoritas ;* " in the first paragraph it is " *Jussus.*"

to reign over that part which had belonged to their father Pippin, and Karloman over that portion which had belonged to their uncle Karloman.[1]

When they had both agreed to these terms, each received that portion of the **kingdom** which had been assigned him. Agreement between the brothers **was** thus established, though **it was only** preserved with the greatest difficulty, since **many** of the friends of Karloman set themselves **to work** to break the friendship, some even going **so far** as to have thoughts of plunging the brothers into civil **war. But** there **was** mor**é** distrust than real danger, **as in the** end proved **to be** the case. For when Karloman died, his **wife, with** his sons and some **of his** chief nobility, slighted **her** husband's brother and fled into Italy, and for no reason whatever placed herself **and** children under the protection **of** Dedier, **King of the Lombards.** Karloman died after **two years of joint** sove-reignty, **when** his brother **Karl,** with the consent **of** all the Franks, **was** made (sole) King.   **771.**

4. I pass by the birth, infancy, and childhood of

---

[1] Karl was crowned, at Noyon, the Austrasian King; Karloman, at Soissons, the Neustrian King.

Karl, because there is no written record concerning
them, nor is any one now known to survive who
can speak from personal knowledge. I have therefore thought it foolish to write about them, and
have given my attention to relating and explaining
those actions, habits, and other portions of his life
which are not matters of uncertainty; first nar-
rating his military exploits at home and abroad;
then his domestic habits and occupations, then his
administration of the kingdom, and lastly, about
his death, omitting nothing that is worthy and
necessary to be narrated.[1]

5. Karl was engaged in many wars. The first
he undertook was the Aquitanian,[2] because there
seemed to be good hope of quickly bringing it
to an end. It had been begun by his father, but
not finished.

His brother at this time was still living, and his
aid was asked. Though King Karl was disappointed
of his brother's assistance, he nevertheless pursued

---

[1] Eginhard's resolve only to relate historical facts and truths.

[2] The Franks had not settled south of the Loire. The conquest
of Aquitania had only been a political conquest. The inhabitants
were a mixture of Basque, Gaul, and Goth. The Kings or Dukes
were nominally subject to the Austrasian king, and were a younger
branch of the Merwings. Waifar was the last, and naturally a
bitter enemy of the Karlings.

the campaign he had undertaken with the greatest
vigour; he would not withdraw from what he had
begun, nor at all desist from the labour of the work,
until by great and long-continued perseverance the
most complete termination had been achieved. He
obliged Hunold,[1] who, after the death of Waifar,
had attempted to seize Aquitain and renew the
war which was almost ended, to flee from the
country and seek refuge in Gascony. Karl, not
being satisfied that he should remain there, crossed
the river Garonne,[2] and by his ambassadors ordered Loup, the King of the Gascons, to give
up the fugitive, adding that if he did not quickly
do so, he would proceed to recover him by force
of arms. Loup wisely surrendered Hunold. He
also placed himself and the province over which
he ruled under the sovereignty of Karl.

6. When the war was finished and affairs settled
in Aquitain—his partner in the government being
now dead—Karl was induced by the prayer and
entreaty of Adrian, Bishop of the city of Rome,
to undertake a war against the Lombards.[3]

---

[1] This Hunold was a mere adventurer.

[2] The Garonne divides the Gascons and the Aquitanians.

[3] The Lombards, "long beards," or "a-long-the-borde" of the
rivers Elbe and Oder, their original settlements, whence they had

His father had undertaken such a war before,
at the request of Pope Stephen, and had met with
much difficulty in the matter, because some of the
chief men of the Franks, his councillors, had been

migrated into Pannonia. The Emperor Justinian **had** countenanced
their passage of the Danube in order to oppose them to the Gepidæ.
After the terrible **war** between **the** Romans and Ostrogoths (535–
553), **which** exterminated the Ostrogoths, and one may almost say
the Romans also, and which **left** Italy depopulated and defenceless,
the Lombards poured in from Pannonia, and transferred their kingdom from the banks of the Danube **to** the plains of the Po. They
also founded two nominally subject, but really independent, Duchies
at Beneventum and Spoleto. Pavia **was** the capital of the kingdom.
On their first settlement in Italy (568), the Lombards were fierce,
savage, and brutal beyond all other barbarians. More than two centuries in a southern climate had somewhat **softened** their manners,
and modified their delight in exhibiting **a** barbarous and loathsome
personal appearance, but **they were** now more than **ever** the secret
terror or actual invaders **of the** Roman State and Church. Luitprand
took Ravenna, and twice appeared with his army before the gates of
Rome. Aistulf, his successor, declared himself the enemy of both
Pope **and Emperor. He** again took Ravenna, which had **been**
recovered **by** the Venetians, put an end to the Greek Exarchate,
and summoned Rome to submit to him. The Popes had discovered
before this how fruitless it was to apply to the Emperor for assistance ; they therefore, **in** their extremity, sought a defender in the
western champion of Christendom. Karl the Hammerer had
received the ambassadors of Pope Gregory II., and listened to their
appeal with attention, but his death prevented him from undertaking an expedition into Italy. His successor, Pippin, was
appealed to by **Pope** Stephen to defend him from Aistulf. Twice
did he lead his army across **the** Alps (755 and 759). On the second
occasion he imposed on Aistulf the conditions mentioned in **the text.**

much opposed to his wishes, and had gone so far as to declare they would desert the King and return home. War had, however, been made against King Aistulf, and had been quickly finished.

There seemed to be a very similar, or rather the same, cause for war to King Karl as there had been to his father. There was not, however, the same difficulty in carrying it out, nor the same result at its conclusion.

Pippin, for his part, after a few days' siege of Pavia, had compelled Aistulf to give hostages, and to restore the fortified towns and castles which he had taken from the Romans, and also to make oath that he would not attempt the recovery of what he restored. Karl, on the other hand, when he had once begun hostilities, did not hold his hand until Dedier, the King, worn out by a long siege, had surrendered at discretion. Adalgis, his son, on whom were fixed the hopes of the nation, was compelled to quit the kingdom and leave Italy altogether. Karl restored to the Romans all that had been forcibly taken from them, and also crushed Hrudogast, Prefect of the parts about Friuli, who was attempting disturbances; and having brought all Italy under his rule, he made his son Pippin King of the conquered territory.

The passage of the Alps into Italy was ex-
773. tremely difficult, and I would have here
related how great was the toil of the
Franks in overcoming the trackless chain of mountains, with peaks towering to the skies, and sharp
and perilous rocks, had it not seemed to me to be
my present task to record the character of the
King's life rather than the incidents of the wars
which he waged.[1]

Suffice it, then, to say that the end of this war
was that Italy was conquered, King Dedier carried
away into perpetual exile, Adalgis, his son, driven
from Italy,[2] and all that had been seized by the

---

[1] Karl mustered his forces for the war at Geneva. He then
divided them, and sent part by the Great S. Bernard pass, under his
uncle Bernhard ; the rest he led himself, by the Mont Cenis pass.
Hannibal had descended into Italy by the Little S. Bernard ;
Napoleon followed the route taken by Karl, having, like him,
assembled his forces at Geneva.

[2] Adalgis went to Constantinople, where the Emperor accorded
him the rank of Patrician. Karl did not destroy the Lombard
Kingdom : he assumed the crown himself.

The celebrated Iron Crown of Lombardy was the gift of Theudelinda, the beautiful and pious queen of Autharis. It is a plain
fillet of gold, set with rubies, emeralds, and sapphires, and lined
with a thin rim of iron, said to be a nail from the true Cross.
It was presented to the cathedral of Monza by Theudelinda, about
the year 590, and still exists in its original form. Napoleon had
himself crowned with this crown when in Italy in 1805. Concerning this, and Karl's Imperial crown and other jewels, see Mr.
King's book on precious stones.

Lombard Kings[1] was restored to Adrian, the rector of the Roman Church.

7. The Lombard war being thus finished, the Saxon war, which seemed for the time to have been neglected, was again renewed. No war undertaken by the Franks was so protracted or so fierce, or so full of toil and hardship, since the Saxons, like most of the nations inhabiting Germany, were naturally brave, and, being addicted to heathenism, were hostile to our religion, and thought it no disgrace to dishonour divine laws or violate human ones.

Causes, too, daily arose which contributed to disturb the peace. The boundaries of their country and ours were in the open almost everywhere contiguous. It was only in a few places that large forests, or ranges of mountains coming between,

[1] That is, the Greek Exarchate. This had been formed on the termination of the Ostrogothic war (553). It was the dominion of the Emperor in Italy, and was governed by his representative, the Exarch. The capital was Ravenna, and the territory corresponded with what was, until a few years ago, the States of the Church. It was the invasion of the Exarchate by Aistulf that brought Pippin into Italy (756). When he had driven Aistulf out, Pippin bestowed his conquest on the Pope. Karl now renewed this grant of territory. It was this celebrated gift of Pippin which laid the foundation of the temporal power of the Pope. It was soon after pretended by the Popes that this act of Pippin's was only a restoration by him of a previous donation by the Emperor Constantine, who had resigned to the Popes the sovereignty of Rome and Italy.

formed a well-defined and **natural** boundary line to **both** countries. **On** the borders therefore, plundering, burning, and bloodshed never **ceased.**[1]

The Franks were so enraged **at this** that they judged **it now to** be no longer a matter of making reprisals, **but so** important **that it** warranted them in undertaking **an** avowed **war against** them. War therefore **was** declared, **and was** carried on

[1] **The Saxons,** "men of **the** seax or dagger." Their settlements were very extensive. Holding the **coast** of the North Sea between the rivers Elbe and Ems, they **extended** southward between those rivers as far as the Thuringian forest **eastward,** and to the confines of the Franks about the Rhine **and Lippe.** The character of the Saxons is described in the text; **but a veil** is drawn over the terrible severity, the blood-shedding, and partial extermination which Karl enacted upon them before he **broke the** Saxon spirit and insured submission. "The true cause," says M. Michelet (" Hist. de France," ii. 39), quoted by Hallam ("Middle Ages," i. 121), "of the Saxon wars, which had been begun under Karl the **Hammerer,** and were in some degree defensive **on the** part of the **Franks, was** the ancient antipathy of the two tribes, enhanced by the growing tendency **to** civilized habit among the latter. **The** Saxons, **in** their deep forests and scantily cultivated plains, **could** not bear **fixed** boundaries of land." Such restrictions were opposed to their barbarian ideas of indefinite territory, and their ancient Teutonic custom of constantly changing their occupancy to **new** pastures. They rejected Christianity, not on its merits, but **as being the** religion of the Saxons' bitterest enemies, **of those who seemed** to them to be the **destroyers of free Teutonic institutions. It was a** war between ancient **Teuton barbarism** and rising Teuton civilization.

This **old** Saxony had nothing in common with the modern diplomatic kingdom, erected **in 1807,** except the name.

continuously **during thirty-three years, with much**
bitterness on both sides, but **with greater**
loss to the Saxons than to the Franks. **It** **772-805.**
was the bad faith **of the Saxons which prevented a**
more speedy termination. **It is hard to say how**
often they were beaten, and humbly **surrendered**
to the King, promising **to** obey his orders, giving **up**
at once the hostages **he** asked, and acknowledging
the ambassadors **sent to them; how** sometimes
they were **so tamed and** compliant as even **to**
promise to give up **their** idolatry, declaring they
wished to **embrace Christianity.** But ready as they
were at times to undertake all these things, they
were always far readier to renounce them. **It is**
difficult to state correctly to which failing they **were**
more prone, since it is certainly the fact that, **after**
the war was begun, scarcely a single year passed in
which they did not **pursue this** shifty **course.**

But **the magnanimity of the** King, and the
unwavering **firmness of his** disposition, alike in
adversity and **prosperity, could not** be shaken
by any faithlessness on **their part, nor could they**
divert him **from his purpose** by tiring **him out.**

He never allowed any **act of insincerity to be**
done with impunity; either **taking the command**
in **person, or** despatching **an army under his**

counts, he took vengeance on their perfidy and exacted from them a commensurate penalty.

He pursued this course until all who continued to resist him were overcome and brought into submission. He then transported ten thousand men, taken from both banks of the Elbe, together with their wives and children, and distributed them here and there, in very small groups, in Gaul and Germany.[1]

It was on the following terms, offered by the King and accepted by the Saxons, that this war, which had lasted so many years, was brought to a close. The Saxons were to put away their heathen worship and the religious ceremonies of their fathers; were to accept the articles of the Christian faith and practice; and, being united to the Franks, were to form with them one people.[2]

---

[1] To Flanders and Brabant, countries which were then only very thinly peopled, where their descendants preserved the same indomitable spirit of resistance to oppression.

[2] That is, the Saxons were to enter the Frankish confederation as the equals of the Franks. This they did, and soon became, with the Franconians, Bavarians, and Swabians, one of the four great nations of the confederation, and their duke one of the Seven Electors. Early in the tenth century the Saxon Duke, Henry Fowler, was elected German King; his son Otto was also King, and in 962 was crowned Emperor. The Saxon Dukes continued to be elected to the Imperial throne until the death of Henry II. in 1024, and were among the most able and powerful of the Teuton Emperors.

8. Although the war lasted so long, the King himself did not fight more than two pitched battles against the enemy, one near a hill called Osneng, near Theotmel,[1] and the other on the river Hasa,[2] both in the same month and at a few days' interval.

783.

In these two battles the enemy were so thoroughly broken in spirit, and beaten, that they no more dared to challenge the King, or to oppose him on his march, except in places where they were protected by fortifications. There fell in this war more of the Frankish nobility, and of those who enjoyed the highest honours, than of their compeers among the Saxons, and it was in its thirty-third year before it was finished.[3]

During those years many great wars sprang up against the Franks in different parts, which were, by the skill of the King, so well managed that it was not without reason that men were perplexed whether to admire more the patience with

---

[1] Detmold.

[2] Near Osnabrück on the river Haase. This place was called in the Middle Ages "Slaughter Hill," *Schlachtvörderberg*, but now *Die Clus.*

[3] Nothing could exceed the fierceness and obstinacy of the war; it is one of the chief events of Karl's reign : if the accounts of the slain on both sides are correct, the bloodshed was almost beyond parallel.

which the King pursued his undertakings, or the good fortune which attended them.

This war was begun **two** years before the Italian war,[1] and although it **was** carried on at the same time without any intermission, there was no relaxation anywhere. In both places the campaign was equally carried on without diminution **of** effort, for, of all contemporary sovereigns, **King Karl** took the highest **rank for his** good administration, and **was most** distinguished for his ability. **In all his** undertakings and enterprises there was nothing **he** shrank from because **of the** toil, and nothing he feared because **of the** danger; but, skilful in weighing everything **at its** true value, he **was** neither yielding .in adversity nor deceived by the smiles of fortune in prosperity.

9. It **was during the time** that the Saxon war **was** being vigorously and incessantly car-**778.** ried **on,** garrisons having been placed in all the most **suitable places on the** borders, that Karl marched into Spain with the best-appointed army possible. Having crossed the Pyrenean mountains, he reduced **all the** fortified towns and castles he came to, and was on his march home with his army

---

[1] **That is,** the Lombard war against Dedier.

and sound, when, in the very pass of the
Pyrenees on his way back, he had a slight experience of Gascon treachery.[1]

The army was moving in column, and its formation was much extended, as the narrowness of the
pass required, when the Gascons, who had placed
ambuscades on the highest ledges of the mountains—the abundant thick cover of wood making
the place most suitable for the disposal of an
ambush—rushed down from their vantage ground
into the valley below, and threw themselves upon
the extreme section of the baggage, and on those
who were marching with it for its protection. The
Gascons attacked them in a hand-to-hand fight,[2]
killed them all to a man, and destroyed the baggage; and being protected by the darkness of the
night, which was then coming on, they quickly
dispersed in all directions.

In this exploit the Gascons were much favoured
by the lightness of their weapons and the nature of
the place where the attack was made, while the
Franks, impeded by their heavy arms and the
unevenness of the ground, were at a great dis-
advantage.[3]

[1] " Wasconiam perfidiam parumper contigit experiri."
[2] " Conserto prælio."
[3] The Spanish expedition was undertaken at the request of a

There were killed in this fight, Eggihard, the
King's Sewer; Anselm, the Pfalsgraf; Roland,[1]
Count of the British March, and many others.[2]
No revenge could be taken at the time for this
defeat, for the enemy immediately dispersed, and so
secretly that no trace was left by which they could
be followed.

10. Karl also brought the Britons into subjection.
They dwelt on the coast in the extreme
779. west of Gaul. They were not obeying the

Saracen Emir, who was aiming at independence of the Caliph
of Cordova, his rightful over-lord. He had made offers of allegiance to Karl, who had to defend his country. By this expedition Karl extended his frontier as far as the Ebro. The country
between that river and the Pyrenees was formed into the Spanish
March.

The Gascons, or Basques, are supposed to be of Turanian origin,
and related to the Fins and Laps, a family quite distinct in speech
from neighbouring Aryan nations, and the only instance of a survival
of any early Turanian occupation of Europe. The Basques dwell-
ing among the fastnesses on both sides of the Pyrenees still main-
tain their national separateness—a bold and hardy race, whose fine
figures and distinctive speech are yet noticeable.

[1] This is the only historical record of the defeat of Roncevaux,
which grew into such marvellous proportions in the romances of the
thirteenth and following centuries, the "Chansons de Roland," etc.
There is an interesting essay on this subject by R. J. King, in his
book of "Sketches and Studies."

[2] Eggihardus, "regiæ mensæ præpositus." Anselmus, "Comes
palatii." Hruodlandus, "Brittannici limitis præfectus."

King's orders, so an expedition was sent against
them, and they were compelled to give hostages
that they would do as they were commanded.[1]

After this the King led his army in person into
Italy, and, passing through Rome, marched
on to Capua, a city of Campania, and, **780.**
pitching his camp there, he threatened to make war
upon the Beneventines unless they submitted to
him.   Aragis, the Duke, avoided this by sending
his sons, Rumold and Grimold, with a large sum of
money, to meet the King.   Aragis asked that his
sons might be accepted as hostages, and promised
that he and his people would obey the King, but
prayed that he himself might be excused from
personal attendance.

The King, having more regard for what was for
the welfare of the people than for the man' obstinacy, granted his request, accepted the hostages
he had sent, and for a large sum of money excused
him from personal attendance.   Only the younger
son of Aragis was detained as a hostage ; the elder
was sent back to his father.   When the ambas-

---

[1] Eginhard mentions in the "Annals," that a great number of
the inhabitants of "Brittannia Insula" fled across the sea on the
invasion of the Angles and Saxons.   They were tributary, though
somewhat unwillingly, to the King of the Franks.

sadors who had come to deliberate upon, and agree
to, the engagements of fidelity to be entered into
by Aragis, on behalf of the Beneventines, had been
dismissed, the King returned to Rome.

Having passed some days there in reverend
visitation of the sacred places of the city, he went
back again into Gaul.

11. The next war was one which sprang up
unexpectedly with the Bavarians. It
787-788.   only lasted for a short time. It was
caused by the arrogance and senselessness of Duke
Tassilo. He had married a daughter of King
Dedier, who thought through her husband to
avenge the exile of her father. Tassilo, being thus
urged on by his wife, made an alliance with the
Huns,[1] whose territories joined those of the
Bavarians on the East, and aimed not only at
independence, but even challenged the King to war.
Karl, unable to brook such immoderate insolence,
moved forward a large army, composed of forces
gathered from all sides and commanded by himself, to the river Lech, determined to obtain satis-
faction from the Bavarians. Having pitched his
camp on the banks of that river, which divides the

---

[1] That is, the Avars.

Bavarians from the Alemanni, **he** resolved to send ambassadors to sound the mind **of the Duke** before he entered their country.[1]

It then seemed that Tassilo did not think that it would be for the advantage of **either** himself or his people to persist in **his** course of action ; he therefore surrendered himself to the King's **clemency, and gave** the hostages demanded— among them **his son** Theodon. **In addition to** this, he pledged his faith **with an** oath that he would **give** no heed **to** any **one** who might attempt **to** persuade him **to revolt** from the King's authority. **It was thus that a** war which had seemed likely to **be a great one** was brought to a speedy termination.

Tassilo, however, being soon after summoned to **appear** before the King, was **not** permitted **to return** ; and the province over which **he** ruled was **no longer** governed by a Duke, but was entrusted to **the charge of** Counts.[2]

---

[1] The Bavarians **had been nominally subject** to the Frankish confederation **from the time of Chlodwig.** This same Tassilo and all the **Bavarian chiefs had taken the** most solemn oaths of allegiance and fidelity **to King Pippin and his sons Karl and** Karloman, swearing **on** the **bodies of** S. Dyonisius and **S.** Martin, pledging themselves, **the whole nation,** and their **successors** for ever. This they had **done at Compiègne (757).**

[2] **By** the extinction **of the** Dukedom, the Bavarians were made

12. When these affairs **had been** thus settled, a war was begun against **those Slavs**[1] whom we

789. are accustomed **to** call **Wiltzi**, but who, according **to** their own pronunciation, are more properly called Welatabi. **In** this war

more trusted members of the Frankish confederation. They became one of the four great nations of the league. It was not long before the Dukedom was revived. In later times, the Bavarians **have** constantly preferred a French alliance to German unity, and **have** ranged themselves by the side of Celtic **levies** against their kindred Teutons. Continuing her policy of supporting the encroachments and aggrandizement of France, **rather** than the real welfare **of** the German people, Bavaria was **erected** into **a** kingdom by Napoleon in 1806. She has, however, lately returned to truer instincts and **a** more legitimate policy, and **done** good service to the Fatherland by assisting in recovering some of its rightful possessions.

The suppression at different times, **by** powerful Emperors, **of some** of the great Dukes- gave **opportunity for** the rise of the **very** numerous lesser German nobility. Karl himself suppressed **all the** great dukes **of** tribes and **nations, as** tending **to strengthen the central government.** In the days of **Karl's** grandsons, they sprang up again as great feudal **and** territorial lords. **Most of the** great fiefs of Gaul **and Germany dated** from the end **of the ninth** century, when they became hereditary in the family then governing them, and very independent of their over-lord.

[1] **Slav,** from *laus*, glory, "the glorious people." Being the latest **wave of** Aryans who pressed into Europe, we therefore find their settlements most to the East. From near the Elbe, and eastward, from the shores of **the Baltic** to the Euxine Sea, was all occupied by different Slavonic tribes—the Wends, the old inhabitants of Prussia; the Lithuanians, Russians, Bohemians, Poles; and much of the country now ruled **by** the Ottoman Turks, on **the** banks of the Danube, **and along** the shores of the Adriatic, contains a Slavic population.

the Saxons fought as our allies, but their allegiance
was rather feigned than real. The cause of the
war was this—the Welatabi could be restrained
by no commands from harassing with constant
invasions the Abodriti, who had long belonged to
the Frankish league.

There is a gulf running in from the Western
Ocean, stretching toward the East ; its length has
not been ascertained, but its breadth nowhere
exceeds one hundred miles, and in many places
it is much narrower.[1] Several nations dwell around
this gulf, such as the Danes and Swedes, whom we
call Northmen, who occupy the northern shores
and all the islands. The southern coasts are held
by the Slavs and Aisti,[2] and other nations ; chief
among these were the Welatabi, against whom the
King was now waging war.

In one expedition under his own command he
so crushed and tamed them, that they resolved to
submit to the uttermost and to refuse nothing.[3]

13. The greatest of all the wars waged by the

[1] The Baltic was little known at this time.

[2] Aisti or Aestyi, Esthonians.

[3] Karl threw two bridges over the Elbe, and harried their
country with fire and sword. Though a warlike people, they were
quite unequal to a contest with the Franks.

King, except the Saxon, was that which now followed, against the Avars or Huns. He set about it with far more ardour and preparation than was bestowed upon any of the others. The King himself only made one expedition into Pannonia—it was that province which the Avar race then inhabited ; the others he entrusted to the direction of his son Pippin, and to the prefects of the provinces, and to the counts and lieutenants. Although these commanders used the greatest exertions, it was not until the eighth year that the war was finished.

789 796.

How many battles were fought, and how much blood shed, is fully attested by the complete depopulation of Pannonia ; even the situation of the royal palace of the Kagan[1] is so obliterated that no trace remains of a human habitation.

In this war the whole nobility of the Avars perished, and the glory of their nation was destroyed. All their riches and treasures, which they had long been accumulating, were carried away, nor can memory recall any war of the Franks in which they have gained greater booty or by which they have been more enriched. Indeed, we may confess that, up to this time, the

---

[1] The Avar chieftain, or king, was so called.

Franks appeared to be a poor nation ; but so much gold and silver was found in the palace, and such a quantity of valuable spoil was taken in the battles, as can scarcely be believed.

The Franks justly spoiled the Huns (Avars) of this booty, for the Huns themselves had no right to it, it being the plunder they had carried off from other nations.

Only two of the chief nobility among the Franks fell in this war—Eric, Duke of Friuli, killed in Liburnia, near Tharsatica, a maritime state,[1] having been cut off by an ambush of the inhabitants ; and Gerold, Prefect of the Bavarians, who was killed in Pannonia, while drawing up his men in line of battle just before engaging the Huns. By whom he was killed is uncertain, since he was slain, with two others who accompanied him, while riding up and down the ranks, and encouraging each man individually.

With these exceptions, the war was almost a bloodless one for the Franks, and although it lasted longer than its magnitude seemed to warrant, its result was most successful.[2]

---

[1] On the Adriatic.

[2] The Avar war was a defensive war, absolutely necessary for the safety of Karl's Empire. Pannonia was an old province of the Roman Empire, lying between the Drave and Danube. This pro-

14. When this and the Saxon war had been brought to an end which their tediousness made

vince, as also Dacia, and other neighbouring lands, were at three different times overrun and occupied by three successive hordes of Asiatics, of the Mongol-Tatar or Turanian family, who, entering Europe by the same road, followed the line of the Danube to the same central position. Though these three invasions are quite distinct, and separated by considerable intervals of time, European writers, distinguishing only the Asiatic character of the invaders, have often confounded them one with another, and given them all the common appellation of Huns, and credited them with a continuous history. Each in turn in the same central position was the scourge of Europe, and the terror alike of the Eastern and Western Empires.

The Scythian cavalry, the Tatar bow and clouds of arrows, made themselves felt in devastating incursions, carried as far as the gates of Constantinople, the plains of the Po, and into the heart of Gaul and Germany. First came the Huns in the fifth century, but after their defeats at Chalons and Netad, they melted away and disappeared from history, and Pannonia was occupied by Lombards and Gepidæ.

Next, the Avars in the sixth century forced their way into the same country. The Gepidæ were obliterated ; the Lombards took North Italy. The Avars possessed themselves of all the country from the Euxine to the Adriatic ; they confined the Eastern Empire to the walls of Constantinople. They were repulsed and driven back within narrower limits, on the one side by the Emperor Maurice in 600, and two hundred years later, on the western side, by the Emperor Karl, who alone has the glory of having been able to contend successfully with these savage Scythians, and of having freed Europe from their wide-spread plundering incursions. Karl penetrated into the very heart of their country, took their "Ring" or royal palace and chief encampment, with all the spoil and booty there collected, and retaliated on that barbarous people some of the calamities they had inflicted on Europe during a period of three acceptable, the two wars which afterwards occurred, one against the Bohemians,[1] and the other against the Linonians,[2] were only of short duration, being quickly finished under the direction of Karl the younger.

The last war undertaken was against the Northmen who are called Danes, who, at first as pirates, and afterwards with a larger fleet, were ravaging the coasts of Gaul and Germany.

810.

hundred years. The nation was cut to pieces. What remained of Avar pride was driven beyond the Danube, and Pannonia was added to the Frankish dominion. No deed of Karl's contributed more to the immediate welfare and safety of Western Europe.

At the end of the ninth century a third Scythian invasion and occupation of Pannonia took place—the Magyar Turks, called by us, Hungarians. Their ravages were as wide-spread and as destructive as their predecessors. They were checked by Henry Fowler at Merseburg, 934, and by the united nations of the German league, under Otto I., at Augsburg, 954. They were then driven back within their present limits. They shortly after accepted the Christian religion, and by degrees adopted the more settled habits and customs of Europeans. Their connexion with the house of Austria dates from the marriage of the Emperor Sigismund with Mary, heiress of Lewis the Great, of Hungary (1383).

It is one of the chief honours of the Hungarians that they opposed an impenetrable barrier to the further advance of the Ottoman Turk in the fifteenth century.—See Gibbon, chap. lv.; Hallam, "Middle Ages," chaps. i. and v.

[1] The Bohemians were a Slavic people. Though not Teutons, they were fully admitted into the German confederation, and their King became one of the seven Electors of the Empire.

[2] Linonia, now Luneburg.

Their King, Godfrey, was puffed up with the delusive hope of making himself master of all Germany, and persisted in regarding Frisia and Saxony as his own provinces. He had already brought the Abodriti under his power and had made them tributary to him.

He even used to boast that he would shortly appear with all his forces at Aachen, where the King's court was held. Foolish as his talk was, there were some who did not altogether discredit him. It was rather thought that he would have attempted something of the kind had not his sudden death prevented him. He was slain by one of his own servants, and thus his own life and the war he had begun were brought to an abrupt conclusion.[1]

15. Such were the wars waged by the most potent prince with the greatest skill and success in different countries during the forty-seven years of his reign. Great and powerful as was the realm

[1] The Danish war was also a defensive war. Godfrey was the head of a Scandinavian confederation of Danes, Norwegians, and Swedes. He had invaded Friesland and Saxony. His assassination terminated the war. The Eyder was now Karl's northern boundary. It is probable that the restraint placed by Karl on the Danes on the land side caused them to become just at this time the pirates of the seas.

of the Franks, which Karl had **received from** his
father Pippin, he nevertheless so splendidly enlarged it by these wars that he almost doubled it.[1]

For previously the Eastern Franks **had only**
inhabited that part of Gaul which lies between the
Rhine and the Loire, the ocean and Balearic **Sea,**
and that part of Germany situated between Saxony
and the Danube, the Rhine **and the Saal,** which
latter river divides the Thuringi from the Sorabi.
The Alemanni and **Bavarians** also belonged **to** the
Frankish confederation. · **But Karl, by the** wars
which have been mentioned, conquered **and** made
tributary, first, **Aquitania and** Gascony, **and** the
whole range of the Pyrenean mountains, **as far as**
the river Ebro, which, rising in Navarre **and flowing**
through the most fertile lands of Spain, **mingles its**
waters **with** the Balearic **Sea** beneath the walls of
Tortosa ; then the whole of Italy, from **Aosta** to
Lower Calabria, where are the boundaries of **the**
Greeks [2] and Beneventines, **an extent of** more **than**

---

[1] Yet none of these were **mere** aggressive wars undertaken for
the sake of conquest.   The Saxon, **Avar, and** Danish were purely
defensive ; Spanish, Lombard, and Wiltz, in defence **of his** allies ;
Aquitanian, Bavarian, Briton, **and Italian,** against revolted subjects

[2] Just the heel and toe of Italy **was all that** now remained to the
Greek Emperors ; afterwards they **regained (890) rather** more, and
held all **south of** the **Bay of** Naples, **and the** promontory of Mount

a thousand miles in length ; then Saxony, which is
indeed no small portion of Germany, and is thought
to be twice as wide as the part where the Franks
dwell, and equal to it in length ; then both
Pannonias, and Dacia which lies on the other bank
of the Danube ; also Istria, Liburnia, and Dalmatia,
with the exception of the maritime towns, which
for friendship's sake, and on account of a treaty, he
allowed the Constantinopolitan Emperor to hold ;
lastly, all the wild and barbarous nations which
inhabit Germany between the Rhine and the
Vistula, the ocean and the Danube, who speak
a very similar language, but are widely different in
manners and dress.   Chief among these were the
Welatabi, Sorabi, Abodriti, and Bæmanni, for with
these there was fighting ; but the rest, who were
more numerous, quietly surrendered.[1]

Garganus, which became a flourishing Greek province. This was
conquered by the Normans between 1030 and 1070.

Sicily remained to the Greeks until it was conquered by the
Saracens, about the middle of the ninth century.   It was conquered
by the Normans between 1060 and 1090.   These two conquests
of the Normans were united under the name of the Kingdom
of Sicily, afterwards the Kingdom of Naples, now part of the
Kingdom of Italy.   Greek, Moor, and Norman have all left their
mark in these countries, where they met, fought, and supplanted
each other.

[1] Slav nations. Bæmanni, *i.e.* Bohemians.

16. The renown of his Kingdom was also much increased by the friendly alliances he cultivated with different kings and nations. Alfonso, King of Gallicia and Asturias,[1] was so bound to him by the ties of friendship that, when he sent him letters or messengers, he used to command that he should be spoken of as being Karl's man. The Kings of the Scots, too, were by his munificence so devoted to his will, that they ever spoke of him as their Lord, and of themselves as his lieges and servants.[2] Letters are still extant from them to him which show that this sort of relationship existed between them.

Haroun,[3] king of the Persians, who, with the

---

[1] Alfonso II., " El Casto."

[2] The Scotch Kings north of the Firth of Forth. Mr. Freeman (" Norman Conquest," vol. i. p. 38) says, " Karl procured the restoration of the banished Northumbrian King, Eardwulf, and there seems reason to believe that both the Northumbrian and his Scottish neighbours acknowledged themselves the vassals of the new Augustus." And again, p. 117, there was "an apparent submission of both Scots and Northumbrians to the Roman Empire in the person of Charles the Great." This is explained at page 560— " The relation both of Scots and Northumbrians seems to have been a relation of *commendation*. The Scots doing homage to Karl on account of his gifts is not unlike the homage which we shall find done by certain French princes to Edward the Confessor."

[3] Haroun-al-Raschid, *the Just* ; his dominion extended from Africa to India. He was the third Caliph of the house of the Abbassides, under whom the seat of the Caliphate was removed to

exception of India, ruled over nearly all the East, was held by the King in such hearty friendship, that he valued Karl's esteem above that of all other Kings and princes of the world, and thought that he alone was worthy to be honoured by his regard and munificence. When the officers sent by King Karl with offerings to the most sacred sepulchre and place of the resurrection of our Lord and Saviour came to Haroun and announced the pleasure of their master, he not only gave them permission to do as they desired, but granted that that revered and sacred spot should be considered as belonging to King Karl.[1] When the ambassadors set out on

Bagdad from Damascus, which had been the seat of government under the house of Ommiad. The early Abbasside Caliphs were the most powerful and most magnificent of all the Mahometan rulers. Constantinople paid an annual tribute to Haroun. In the year 755 Abd-al-Rahman, a prince of the dethroned house of Ommiad, put himself at the head of the Mahometans of Spain, and established the independence of the Caliph of Cordova. Thus the Caliphate, like the Christian Empire, was divided into the Eastern and Western portions, the ruler of each giving himself out as, and claiming to be, the rightful successor to and Lord of the whole. In the darkest ages of Christian Europe, the court and city of Cordova were greatly distinguished for their learning and refinement, for their patronage of letters and art, and the promotion of science and liberal studies. Even amid the bright light of the fifteenth century, the overthrow of Granada was a distinct loss to Europe.

[1] The Eastern Caliph, though the enemy of the Eastern Emperor, was the ally of the Western Emperor, their dominions being too

their return, he sent with them his own envoys, who conveyed to the King strange and curious gifts, with garments and spices and other rich products of the East, just as he had sent him a few years before, upon his request, the only elephant he then possessed.[1]

The Constantinopolitan Emperors, Nicephorus, Michael, and Leo, of their own accord, also sought his friendship and alliance, and sent to him several embassies ; and since by assuming the Imperial title he had laid himself open to the grave suspicion of wishing to deprive them of Empire, he made with them the most binding treaty possible, that

far apart for hostile rivalry ; for the same reason, the Western Caliph at Cordova was the natural ally of Constantinople.

[1] The name of the elephant was Abulabaz. It arrived at Pisa in the summer of 801, the year Karl was in Italy. A fleet was prepared to transport the animal into Gaul, but for some reason or other the fleet put back in October, and, the Alps being covered with snow, it had to winter at Vercellæ, and did not arrive at Aachen until August the following year. It was under the charge of one Isaac, a Jew. Unfortunately, Abulabaz died suddenly when with Karl on the Danish expedition in 810.

Among the other gifts, the "ingentia dona," sent by Haroun, were a splendid pavilion of different colours, and a water clock, which must have been as great a marvel as the clock at Strasburg. Golden balls fell down at the completion of the hours, and twelve knights came out of as many doors, and the hour was sounded on cymbals.

Haroun-al-Raschid is the Caliph of the "Arabian Nights."

there might be no occasion of offence between
them.   But the Romans and Greeks always viewed
with distrust the power of the Franks; hence arose
the Greek proverb, "Have a Frank for a friend
but not for a neighbour." [1]

[1] The Empire, transported to Constantinople in 325, still continued to be a thoroughly Latin Empire until after the death of
Justinian, in 565.   It was always the *Roman Empire*, but in the
time of Leo III., the Isaurian (718–741). The Greek tongue had quite
superseded Latin.   Greek in language, habits, and dress, though still
calling themselves Romans, the rest of the world spoke of them
as the Greeks, and the Empire as the Greek or Eastern Empire, as it
now extended only over Greek-speaking people, thus distinguishing
it from the Latin or Western Empire.   Though much corrupted by
the lower orders and very debased in the provinces, the Greek
language was spoken and written with great purity of idiom among
the rich and refined at Constantinople, until the taking of the city
by the Turks (1453).   Until the end of the tenth century it
remained the language of the liturgy of Lower Calabria.   The
revival of the study of Greek in Italy in the fourteenth century was
assisted by professors from Constantinople.

The Emperors at Constantinople sullenly acquiesced in what
they were powerless to resist, and addressed the Emperor in
the West as their brother, or denounced him as a usurper, as
their pride or their interests moved them.   Though we speak, of
very necessity's sake, of the Eastern and Western Empire, no such
real division of the Roman Empire was aimed at by Karl and Pope
Leo, or indeed thought to be possible.   The Roman Empire was
one and indivisible.   Karl aimed at—indeed, had long been aiming
at—the world's crown.   The Pope looked again to make Rome, this
time Christian Rome, the centre of the Empire and the head of Christendom.   The Imperial throne was actually vacant, and the Pope
and Romans claimed to have elected and crowned, and Karl

17. Illustrious as the King was in the work of enlarging his Kingdom and in conquering foreign nations, and though so constantly occupied with such affairs, he nevertheless began in several places very many works for the advantage and beautifying of his Kingdom. Some of these he was able to finish. Chief among them may be mentioned, as deserving of notice, the Basilica of the Holy Mother of God, built at Aachen, a marvel of workmanship; and the bridge over the Rhine at Mainz, five hundred paces in length, so broad is the river at that place.[1] This bridge, however, was destroyed by fire the year before the King died, nor could it be restored on account of his approaching death,

claimed to be, the sole Lord of the Roman Empire and the rightful successor of Constantine VI. Constantinople continued to elect Emperors until taken by the Turks, 1453, not of the Eastern half of the Empire, but of the whole Empire, repudiating the election of Karl and his successors as invalid.

The one, universal, and Catholic character of the Roman Empire, as it did always, and still continued to present itself to men's minds, prevented Karl from ever entertaining any idea of a division of what was held to be indivisible. In actual fact, a rival line of Emperors thwarted Karl's scheme, but that did not destroy in men's minds the theory of the unity of the Roman Empire, which remained as strong as ever. In speech men had to adapt their expressions to actual facts, and distinguish between East and West.

[1] The Rhine at Mainz is 1469 feet in breadth, one of the widest places; under the present bridge of boats may be seen remnants of pillars said to be those of Karl's bridge.

although it was in the King's mind to replace the
wooden structure by a bridge of stone.

He also began some magnificent palaces, one
not far from Mainz, near the village of Ingelheim,
and another at Nymeguen, on the river Waal,
which flows past the island of the Batavians on
the southern side. He was more especially particular in giving orders to the priests and fathers to
see to the restoration of those churches under their
care, which in any part of his Kingdom he found had
fallen into decay, taking care by his officers that
his commands were obeyed. He also constructed
a fleet for the war against the Northmen.[1] For
this purpose ships were built on the rivers of Gaul
and Germany which flow into the North Sea. As
the Northmen were making a practice of ravaging
the coasts of Gaul and Germany with constant
harryings, he posted towers and outlooks in all the
harbours, and at the mouths of those rivers which
ships could navigate. By these defences he prevented any enemy from being able to pass. He
did the same thing in the south, on the coast of the
provinces of Narbonne and Septimania, and all
along the coast of Italy as far as Rome, for in

[1] The great Alfred also found that a good fleet was the only
security against the northern pirates.

those parts the Moors had lately **taken to piracy.
Thus Italy suffered** no great damage from the
Moors, nor Gaul **or Germany from** the **North-**
men, during the reign of Karl, except that Civita
Vecchia, a city **of** Etruria, was betrayed to the
Moors, who took it and destroyed it, and **in** Frisia
some islands off **the German coast** were plundered
by the Northmen.[1]

18. **Such does it appear was the** character **of the**
King, in **defending, enlarging, and** beautifying his
Kingdom, and **one** must **be permitted to admire
his mental gifts and his** great **firmness of purpose**
in all circumstances, whether **of prosperity or
adversity.**

I **will now begin to speak of** other **matters
relating to his private and domestic** life. **On the**
death of his father **he bore all the** jealousy **and ill-
will** of his brother, **in the division** of the Kingdom,
with so much patience and forbearance that he
astonished everybody, **for he would not allow himself even to be provoked to anger by him.**

It **was by the** desire of **his mother that he took**

---

[1] In these days there were three great enemies to the security
of life and property in Europe—the Avars (and afterwards the
Hungarians), the robbers on the land ; the Northmen, the pirates of
the North Seas ; and the Moors, the pirates of the Mediterranean.

for his wife a daughter of **Dedier, King of the**
Lombards; **but at** the end **of a year he divorced**
her, **for what reason** is uncertain. He then married
Hildegard, a Swabian lady of **noble birth,** by
whom he had three sons, Karl, Pippin, and Ludwig,
and three daughters, Hruodrud, Berthrad, and
Gisla. He had also three other daughters, Theo-

THE FAMILY OF THE EMPEROR KARL.

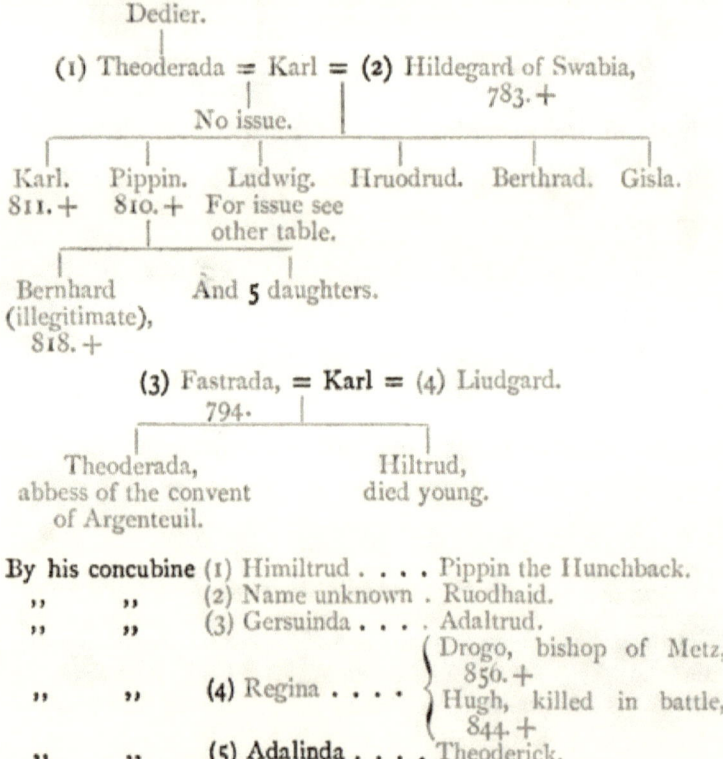

Dedier.

(1) Theoderada = Karl = (2) Hildegard of Swabia,
783. +

No issue.

Karl.   Pippin.   Ludwig.   Hruodrud.   Berthrad.   Gisla.
811. +   810. +   For issue see
other table.

Bernhard   And **5** daughters.
(illegitimate),
818. +

(3) Fastrada, = Karl = (4) Liudgard.
794.

Theoderada,   Hiltrud,
abbess of the convent   died young.
of Argenteuil.

By his concubine (1) Himiltrud . . . . Pippin the Hunchback.
   ,,   ,,   (2) Name unknown . Ruodhaid.
   ,,   ,,   (3) Gersuinda . . . . Adaltrud.
   ,,   ,,   (4) Regina . . . . { Drogo, bishop of Metz, 856. +
                                           { Hugh, killed in battle, 844. +
   ,,   ,,   (5) Adalinda . . . . Theoderick.

derada and Hiltrud by his wife Fastrada, a German
of the Eastern Franks, and Ruodhaid by a concubine whose name I do not remember. On the
death of Fastrada he married Liudgard, of the
Alemanni nation. She bore him no children.
After her death he had three concubines, Gersuinda, of the Saxon nation, by whom he had
a daughter named Adaltrud ; Regina, who bore him
Drogo and Hugh ; and Adalinda, who had a son
named Theoderick. His mother Berthrad lived
with him to old age, in great honour, being looked
up to by her son with the greatest respect, so that
no difference ever arose between them, except with
regard to the divorce of the daughter of King
Dedier, whom she had persuaded him to marry.
She did not die until after the death of Hildegard,
having lived to see three grandsons and as many
grand-daughters in the house of her son. She was
buried by the King with much honour in the·church
of S. Dionysius,[1] where his father had been laid.
He had one sister, Gisla, who was dedicated to
a religious life from her earliest years. Like his
mother, she was regarded by the King with the
greatest affection. She died a few years before him,
and was buried in the convent to which she had
retired.

[1] S. Denis, near Paris.

19. The King thought so much about the education of his children that he caused both sons and daughters to be early instructed in those liberal studies which attracted his own attention.[1]   As

[1] **Learning was** at a very low ebb. It had been declining, with the gradual disuse of Latin, ever since the beginning of the fifth century ; it continued to decline until after the tenth. The Latin tongue, in which was all the history, learning, and knowledge of the past **ages,** could now only be read by a very few. Greek in the West **was** altogether unknown. Any little learning there was, was preserved and buried in the monasteries. **Books** were scarce ; the only libraries were those in religious houses, where the works of antiquity lay on the shelves unread, to be exhumed in after ages. Secular learning was discouraged by the clergy, **while** Christianity had yielded no literature capable of enlightening or cultivating its professors. Writing materials were certainly scarce and expensive. The same depth of ignorance was not reached by all countries at the same period, else the lamp of learning had **quite** gone out. Gaul and Germany lay under the greatest darkness during the **two** centuries (600–800) preceding the reign **of** Karl, who, by founding schools and collecting together the most learned men, made a noble attempt to lift the cloud.

Gaul, as a Roman **province in the** fifth century, before the invasion of the Franks, **was** more polished and cultivated than it was **any** time after, until the tenth century. The sixth was the very worst century in every respect that Italy ever saw. England, redeemed by **a** few men of letters in the seventh **and** eighth, was most benighted in the ninth century. Yet **in the** latter of these centuries, the darkest ages of Christendom, Cordova possessed a library of six hundred thousand volumes, and other cities of the Caliph were proportionately rich. There the philosophers of Greece were eagerly read, and the study of medicine, mathematics, architecture, and astronomy **was** diligently cultivated. Many Jews and

soon as his sons were old enough **he** caused them
to ride on horseback, as was the Frankish custom,
and to practise themselves in arms and hunting.
He bade his daughters should learn wool-spinning
and the use **of** the distaff and spindle, and **be**
taught to employ themselves industriously in every
virtuous occupation, that they might **not** be ener-
vated by idleness.

Of this large family, **two sons and one daughter**
died before him—Karl, **the** eldest, and Pippin,
whom he had made **King of Italy,** and Hruodrud,
his eldest girl, who **had** been betrothed to Constantine VI., the Emperor of the Greeks. Pippin left
surviving one son, Bernhard, and five daughters,
Adalhaid, Atula, Guntrada, Berthaid, and **Theo-**
derada. The King showed marked tokens of his
affection toward them, allowing his grandson to
succeed to his father's Kingdom, and bringing up
his grand-daughters with **his** own daughters. He
bore the deaths **of his** sons and daughters with that
greatness **of soul for which he was** distinguished ;
but his resignation was **not** greater than his affection, for he mourned for them **with** tears. So also,

Christians resorted **to** Cordova to assist in translating Greek authors.
See Gibbon, chap. viii. ; also Mr. Freeman's "History of the
Saracens," **Lecture v.,** where there **is a most** interesting sketch of
Arabic learning.

when the death of Adrian, the Roman Pontiff,[1] was announced to him, regarding him as his chief friend, he wept for him as if he had lost the son or brother that was dearest to him. For he was most sincere in his friendships, being readily open to form them and most constant in retaining them, cherishing with the most sacred regard those whom he had united to himself in ties of affection.

He was so careful in the bringing up of his sons and daughters that when at home he never dined without them, and they always accompanied him on his journeys, his sons riding by his side, and his daughters following close behind, attended by a train of servants appointed for that purpose. His daughters were very fair, and he loved them passionately. Strange to say, he would never consent to give them in marriage, either to any of his own nation or to foreigners; but he kept them all at home and near his person at all times until his death, for he used to say that he could not deprive himself of their society. On account of this, although happy in all else, he here experienced the malignity of fortune; but he concealed his vexation,

---

[1] The different expressions used by Eginhard for the Pope are —"Romanus Pontifex," "Romanæ ecclesiæ Rector," "Papa," "Romanæ urbis Episcopus."

and conducted himself as if they had never given
rise to injurious suspicions, and as if no reports had
ever gone abroad concerning them.[1]

20. He had also by one of his concubines
another son, Pippin, whom I have omitted to mention among the others ; he had a good countenance,
but was deformed by a hunch back. When his
father was wintering in Bavaria, being detained
there by the war against the Huns, this son Pippin
pretended sickness, and formed a conspiracy against
the King, together with some of the chief men of
the Franks, who had seduced him with the foolish
hope of making him King. The plot being discovered and his fellow conspirators punished,
Pippin's hair was shorn off, and he was allowed
to pass his time in religious exercises in the
abbey at Pruhm. To this he readily consented.
Another dangerous conspiracy against the King
had been set on foot before in Germany. Some of
its authors were condemned to the loss of their
eyes, others saved their limbs, but all were
exiled. None, however, were put to death, except

[1] See M. Guizot's " History of Civilization in Europe," Lecture
xxiii., where is discussed the supposed marriage of Eginhard with
Emma.

three, who drew their swords in defence against those sent to take them, and went so far as to kill some of them. These were slain because there was no other way of dealing with them.[1]

It is thought that in both instances the cruelty of Queen Fastrada was the original cause of these conspiracies against the King, and he seems to have departed very far from the usual gentleness and clemency of his natural disposition in permitting the Queen's inhumanity. The King himself during all his life was regarded by all men, both at home and abroad, with such love and affection that he, at least, was never charged by any one with wanton cruelty.

21. He had a great fondness for foreigners, and was so anxious to entertain them that their great numbers became an improper burden, not merely to the palace, but even to the Kingdom. The King, however, in keeping with his generosity, was very little oppressed by any such thoughts, since a reputation for liberality and the reward of renown well compensated such inconveniences.

---

[1] Faithless vassals and rebel lords seem to have been dealt with very leniently, compared with the practice of later times, when the least suspicion of treason cost a man his head.

22. The person of **Karl was** large and robust, **and** of commanding stature,[1] though not exceeding good proportions, for it appears that he measured seven feet in height. **The** top of his head was round, his eyes large and animated, his nose some-**what** long, his hair white, and his face bright and pleasant ; so that, whether standing or sitting, **he** showed **very** great presence and dignity. Although his neck was thick and rather short, **and his** belly too prominent, still the fair proportions of his limbs concealed these defects. His walk **was firm,** and the whole carriage of his body was manly. His voice **was clear, but not** so strong as his frame would have **led one to expect.** His health was good until the last **four** years of his life, when he was attacked with frequent fevers, and latterly walked **lame on** one foot. Even in illness he leaned more on his own judgment than on the advice of physicians, whom he greatly disliked, because they used to recommend him to **leave off** roasted meats, which **he** preferred, **and to accustom himself to** boiled.

He took **constant exercise in** riding and hunting,

---

[1] " Statura eminenti," "tamen justam non excederet mensuram." A "justa statura" was reckoned among the Romans at six feet. Seven feet was the "summus modus." The Teutons are thought to have been a taller race ; the Burgundians were said to be fre-quently seven feet.

which was natural for a Frank, since scarcely any
nation can be found to equal them in these pursuits.
He also delighted in the natural warm baths, fre-
quently exercising himself by swimming, in which
he was very skilful, no one being able to outstrip
him.   It was on account of the warm baths there
that he built the palace at Aachen,[1] living there
constantly during the last years of his life and
until his death. He not only invited his sons to
bathe with him, but also his chief men and friends,
and occasionally even a crowd of his attendants and
guards, so that at times one hundred men or more
would be bathing together.

23. He wore the dress of his native country—
that is, the Frankish ; on his body a linen shirt
and linen drawers; then a tunic with a silver
border, and stockings. He bound his legs with
garters and wore shoes on his feet. In the
winter he protected his shoulders and chest with a
vest made of the skins of otters and sable. He
wore a blue cloak, and was always girt with his
sword, the hilt and belt being of gold and silver.

---

[1] The warm springs here were well known to the Romans, who
called the town Aquæ Grani. Remains of Roman baths have
been found near the Minster and Elisenbrunnen.

Sometimes he wore a jewelled sword, but only on great festivals, or when receiving foreign ambassadors. He thoroughly disliked the dress of foreigners, however fine, and he never put it on except at Rome—once at the request of Pope Adrian, and again a second time, to please his successor, Pope Leo. He then wore a long tunic, chlamys, and shoes made after the Roman fashion. On festivals he used to walk in processions clad in a garment woven with gold, and shoes studded with jewels, his cloak fastened with a golden clasp, and wearing a crown of gold set with precious stones.[1] At other times his dress differed little from that of a private person.

24. In his eating and drinking he was temperate ; more particularly so in his drinking, since he had the greatest abhorrence of drunkenness in anybody, but more especially in himself and his companions. He was unable to abstain from food for any length

---

[1] The Imperial crown of Karl the Great, which was the crown afterwards used at the coronation of the Roman Emperors as long as they existed, is octagonal, of eight upright plaques of gold with rounded tops, studded with jewels. From the centre plaque rises a Greek cross, also jewelled. An arched rib like a flying buttress connects the cross with the plaque at the back. It is Byzantine workmanship. It is now, rather out of place, in the Imperial library at Vienna.

of time, and often complained that fasting was
injurious to him. He very rarely feasted, only on
great festive occasions, when there were very large
gatherings. The daily service of his table was only
furnished with four dishes, in addition to the roast
meat, which the hunters used to bring in on spits,
and of which he partook more freely than of any
other food.

While he was dining he listened to music or
reading. History and the deeds of men of old
used to be read. He derived much pleasure from
the works of St. Augustine, especially from his
book called " Civitas Dei." He took very spar-
ingly of wine and other drinks, rarely taking at
meals more than two or three draughts. In summer, after the mid-day repast, he would take some
fruit and one draught, and then, throwing aside
his clothes and shoes as at night, he would repose
for two or three hours. He slept at night so lightly
that he would break his rest four or five times, not
merely by awaking, but even getting up.

While he was dressing and binding on his sandals,
he would receive his friends ; and also, if the Count
of the palace announced that there was any cause
which could only be settled by his decree, the
suitors were immediately ordered into his presence,

and, as if sitting in court, he heard the case and
gave judgment. And this was not the only business that used to be arranged at that time, for
orders were then given for whatever had to be
done on that day by any officer or servant.

25. He was ready and fluent in speaking, and
able to express himself with great clearness. He
did not confine himself to his native tongue,[1] but
took pains to learn foreign languages, acquiring
such knowledge of Latin that he used to repeat his
prayers in that language as well as in his own.
Greek he could better understand than pronounce.
In speaking he was so voluble that he almost
gave one the impression of a chatterer.[2] He
was an ardent admirer of the liberal arts, and
greatly revered their professors, whom he promoted
to high honours. In order to learn grammar, he
attended the lectures of the aged Peter of Pisa,
a deacon ; and for other instruction he chose as his
preceptor Albinus, otherwise called Alcuin,[3] also

---

[1] His native tongue was Low German.

[2] " Didascalus appareret."

[3] Alcuin (*Anglicè*, Ealhwine), born at York (734), and therefore
a Northumbrian, and an Angle or Englishman. Eginhard is
incorrect in speaking of him as " Saxonici generis homo." On the
frequent misuse of the term " Saxon," see Mr. Freeman's " Norman

a deacon—a Saxon by race, from Britain, the most
learned man of the day, with whom the King spent
much time in learning rhetoric and logic, and more
especially astronomy.　He learned the art of com-
putation, and with deep thought and skill very
carefully calculated the courses of the planets.

Karl also tried to write, and used to keep his
tablets and writing-book under the pillow of his
couch, that when he had leisure he might practise
his hand in forming letters ; but he made little
progress in a task too long deferred, and begun too
late in life.[1]

26. The Christian religion, in which he had been
brought up from infancy, was held by Karl as most
sacred, and he worshipped in it with the greatest
piety.　For this reason he built at Aachen a most
beautiful church, which he enriched with gold and
silver, and candlesticks, and also with lattices and

Conquest," vol. i. p. 530.　Ealhwine, in accordance with the con-
ceit of the Middle Ages, assumed the name of Albinus Flaccus.
The school at York was at this time very flourishing.　Ealhwine
had been to Rome to obtain the pallium for Albert, Archbishop of
York, and probably met with Karl in Italy.　He became chief
of the school attached to Karl's court, and assisted in organizing
the public schools throughout the realm.

[1] To be able to write, even to sign their names, was at this time
a rare accomplishment for laymen, however exalted in rank.

doors of solid brass. When columns and marbles
for the building could not be obtained from elsewhere, he had them brought from Rome and
Ravenna.

As long as his health permitted, he was most
regular in attending the church at matins and
evensong, and also during the night, and at the time
of the Sacrifice ; and he took especial care that all
the services of the church should be performed in
the most fitting manner possible, frequently caution-
ing the sacristans not to allow anything improper
or unseemly to be brought into, or left in, the
building.

He provided for the church an abundance of
sacred vessels of gold and silver, and priestly vest-
ments, so that when service was celebrated it was
not necessary even for the doorkeepers, who are the
lowest order of ecclesiastics, to perform their duties
in private dress. He carefully revised the order of
reading and singing, being well skilled in both,
though he did not read in public, nor sing, except
in a low voice and only in the chorus.

27. He was most devoted in providing for the
poor, and in charitable gifts, which the Greeks call
almsgiving. In this matter he took thought not

only for those of his own country and kingdom, but also for those whom he heard were living in poverty beyond the seas, in Africa, Egypt, and Syria, at Carthage, Alexandria, and Jerusalem, to whom he used to send money in compassion for their wants. It was on this account especially that he courted the friendship of foreign princes, that he might be able to become a solace and comfort to those Christians who were living under their rule.

He held the church of the blessed Peter the Apostle, at Rome, in far higher regard than any other place of sanctity and veneration, and he enriched its treasury with a great quantity of gold, silver, and precious stones.[1]

To the Pope he made many and rich presents ; and nothing lay nearer his heart during his whole reign than that the city of Rome [2] should attain to

---

[1] Many of these would probably be old engraved gems, which had seen Rome centuries before. Precious stones were little valued by the Greeks and Romans until they had been engraved.

[2] Rome fell to the second place among the cities of the Empire on the removal of the seat of government to Constantinople in 323, and was still further degraded to the second place in Italy when the seat of the Exarch was fixed at Ravenna, in 553. The city had continued to be rich and prosperous, and the houses of her chief nobility magnificent and luxurious, for two hundred years after the removal of the seat of the Empire. After that it rapidly declined, and reached its lowest state of wretchedness and misery at the

its ancient importance by his zeal and patronage,
and that the church of S. Peter should, through him,
not only be in safe keeping and protection, but
should also by his wealth be ennobled and enriched
beyond all other churches.   Although he thought

end of the sixth century, when it was deserted by all except a crowd
of miserable herdsmen and paupers. When the Goths took the
city (411), they carried away all the precious movables of gold and
silver, the gems and jewels, public and private, with the exception
only of the sacred vessels in the churches.   The Vandals (455)
carried off all the valuable statuary and heavier movables, not
sparing the churches.   The spoils of the Goths, " the Nibelungen
hoard," was dispersed through the cities of Gaul and Spain.   Much
of it fell into the hands of the Franks, and went to enrich the shrines
of Frankland.   The spoils of the Vandals were lost through a storm
in the Mediterranean.

In the wars between Belisarius and the Ostrogoths (535-553)
Rome was almost depopulated, and though most of her public
buildings survived, they fell into decay and ruin. Civic strife,
wanton destruction, and the practice of using the old buildings as
materials for making new ones, wrought far greater destruction than
the barbarian invaders had done.   After the return of the Popes
from their exile at Avignon, in 1378, Rome revived ; the old nobles
returned, new families sprang up, the kinsmen of the Popes, and the
city began to be rebuilt.   In the fifteenth century and beginning
of the sixteenth, under the Popes of the house of Medici, and other
patrons of art, Rome again became for the second time the finest city
of the world—the centre of the greatest efforts of the Renaissance :
magnificent churches, S. Peter's rebuilt, sculptured porticoes,
painted ceilings, the houses of the nobility beautifully decorated
within and without, and the noblest works of antiquity boldly
rivalled.   See concluding chapter of Gibbon's " Roman Empire."

G

so much of this, it was only **four times,** during the forty-seven years of his reign, **that** he had leisure to go to Rome **for** prayer and supplication.[1]

28. The last visit he paid to Rome was not only **for the** above reasons, but also because **the** Romans had driven Pope Leo to ask his assistance—for they had grievously ill-treated **him;** indeed, **his** eyes had been plucked out and his tongue cut off.[2]

Karl therefore went **to** Rome, and stayed there the whole winter in **order** to reform and quiet **the** Church, which was in a most disturbed state. It was at this **time** that he received

800.

---

[1] Karl **visited** Rome—in the **winter of** 773-4, on the occasion of the Lombard war **;** in the winter of 780-1, for prayer and supplication : on this occasion his **two** sons were crowned **by** Pope Adrian—Pippin King of Italy, and Ludwig King of Aquitain ; in the winter of 786-7, to receive the submission of the Beneventines ; in the winter of 800-1, **to** quell disturbances in the **city, and to** reform the Church. He was then crowned Emperor.

[2] The election of Leo to the Papacy had not been popular. The nephews of the late Pope put themselves at the head of a sedition. Leo was attacked when in a solemn procession to the church of S. Lorenzo, at Luana, thrown from his horse, wounded, and left for dead. But his injuries do not seem to have been of so deep **or permanent a** character as the text describe, or they did need the reported miracle to recover speech and sight. He escaped to Spoleto, and made his way to Karl at Paderborn. Karl sent him back to Rome with the protection of a strong escort, and promised to come himself in the following year.

the title of Emperor and **Augustus, to which** at
first he was so averse that he remarked **that had he**
known the intention of the Pope, he would not **have**
entered the church **on that day, great festival**
though it was.[1]

He bore **very quietly the** displeasure **of the**
Roman Emperors, **who were** exceedingly **indignant**
at his assumption **of** the Imperial title, **and over-**
came their sullenness by his great magnanimity, in
which, without doubt, **he** greatly excelled them,
sending them frequent embassies, and styling them
his brothers in his letters **to them.**

29. **After he** had taken **the** Imperial **title, he**
turned his attention **to the laws of his** people,
which seemed greatly to need **it, since the** Franks
have two laws,[2] which differ **much in** many
places.

---

[1] This remark **of Karl's seems a** little at variance with the evident
object of his **ambition. He may have** thought that the Pope had
acted too precipitately, **and that further** negotiations with the Con-
stantinopolitans might **have resulted in** obtaining a better title than
the Pope and Romans **in Rome could bestow.**

[2] That is, the laws of the Salian Franks **and** the laws of the
Ripuarian Franks. The Salian was the earliest collection of
Frankish customs, and probably had some definite existence before
the great Frankish conquests under Chlodwig. It was essen-
tially a penal code, dealing with crimes of robbery and violence,

Karl's intention was to add what was wanting
in each, to assimilate discrepancies, and to correct
what was mischievous and wrongly expressed.   In
the end, however, he did nothing more than add a
few capitularies, and those imperfect ones.

He, however, caused the unwritten laws, of all
the nations under his rule, to be tabulated and
reduced to writing.   He also wrote out and committed to memory the rude and very ancient
songs[1] which told of the exploits and wars of the
kings of old. He also began a grammar of the
speech of his country.[2]   He also gave names in
the national tongue to the months of the year, for
up to this time the Franks had distinguished them

and fixing the "wehrgeld" or price of blood, the money composition to be paid to a murdered man's friends, according to his rank,
by the murderer.   When, in the fourteenth century, the Salic law,
a provision of which declared that " Salic lands shall not fall to
women ; the inheritance shall devolve only in males," was invoked
to bar claims to the French crown, it had become obsolete, and
had been forgotten for more than four centuries.

The Ripuarian was probably not so ancient a collection of
customs, and only reached a definite form in the reign of Dagobert
(628-638).   It was more influenced by Roman customs, and was less
barbarous than the earlier Salic.

Both laws expressly stated that the Romans living under Frankish
rule were to be tried by Roman law, that is, by the Theodosian Code.

[1] " Barbara et antiquissima carmina," the old songs of heathen
times.

[2] " Patrii sermonis "—German.

partly by Latin and partly by barbarian names.
He likewise gave the proper names to the twelve
winds, for previously names were known for hardly
four.

The month January he called Wintarmanoth ;
February, Hornung ; March, Lentrinmanoth ; April,
Ostarmanoth ; May, Winnemanoth ; June, Brach-
manoth ; July, Heuvimanoth ; August, Aranma-
noth ; September, Witumanoth ; October, Windu-
memanoth ; November, Herbistmanoth ; December,
Heilagmanoth.   And the winds thus : that called
in Latin Subsolanus, he named Ostroniwint ; Eurus,
Ostsunderen ; Euroauster, Sundostren ; Auster,
Sundren ; Austroafricus, Sundwestren ; Africus,
Westsundren ; Zephyrus, Westren ; Chorus, West-
nordren ; Circius, Nordwestren ; Septentrio, Nordren ; Aquilo, Nordostren ; Vulturnus, Ostnorden.

30. Towards the close of his life, when bowed
down by disease and old age, he summoned to
him his son Ludwig, the King of Aquitain, who
alone survived of the sons of Hildegard, and in a
solemn assembly of the chief men of the whole
realm of the Franks, and with their unanimous
consent, appointed Ludwig his partner in the
whole Kingdom and heir of the Imperial Title.   He

then placed the royal crown on his head and bade
that he be saluted as Emperor and Augustus.[1]

This proposal was received by all who were
present with great approbation. It seemed

813. to them as if Heaven inspired the King in
advancing the prosperity of the Kingdom, for this
arrangement increased his own dignity and struck
foreign nations with no slight awe.

The King then dismissed his son into Aquitain,
and, although weakened by age, went on his usual
hunting expedition in the neighbourhood of the
palace at Aachen. In this pursuit he passed the
remainder of the autumn, and returned to Aachen
early in November. During the winter, in the
month of January, he was confined to his bed by a
sharp attack of fever. He at once prescribed for
himself a lowering diet, which was his usual treat-
ment of fever, thinking that by this means he
could throw off the disease, or at least control it;
but inflammation of the side, which the Greeks call
pleurisy, supervened. He still continued to starve
himself, only keeping himself up by occasionally
taking liquids; and on the seventh day after he had
been confined to his bed he received the Holy

---

[1] This was at Aachen, 813. At the same time Bernhard, son of
Pippin, was made King in Italy.

Communion, and died soon after, at nine o'clock, on the 28th January, in the seventy-third year of his age and forty-seventh of his reign.

31. His body was reverently **washed** and tended, and then carried **into the** church and buried, to the great grief **of all** his people. **There** 814. was some doubt **at first where was the most proper** place for his burial, for during his life **he had given no orders** on this matter. **At last it was agreed by** all **that he** could be buried **in** no more fitting place **than in the church** which **he had built at his** own cost at Aachen, out **of love to** God and our Lord **Christ, and** to the honour of the ever blessed Virgin, **His** Mother.[1] So he was buried there on the same

---

[1] The church **at** Aachen consists of **two parts** erected at different times in entirely different styles. The earlier part, built by Karl, **is the** oldest authentic example of its style, and the most important building of its class in Europe. The nave, externally a sixteen-sided polygon about 105 feet in diameter, consists internally of an octagon surmounted **by** a dome, 47 feet 6 inches in diameter, sup-**ported** by eight piers. It measures 105 feet in height, and is divided **into four stages. The** two lower galleries, running over **the** side aisles, **are covered** with bold intersecting **vaults ; the third,** like the triforium of later churches, **is** open to the roof ; above **it** are eight **windows, which** give light to the central **dome.** To the west of this **is a tower** flanked on either side by a semicircular turret, and to the **east was a** semicircular apse, containing the high altar, pulled down in 1353. **These form** the church erected **by** Karl, 774-804. **The** works were superintended by Eginhard, **and** the building conse-

day that he died.   Above **his** tomb was erected **a** gilded monument, with his effigy and title upon it. His dignity was thus described—

UNDER **THIS TOMB** IS PLACED **THE BODY OF** KARL, THE GREAT AND ORTHODOX EMPEROR, WHO GLORIOUSLY ENLARGED THE REALM OF THE FRANKS, **AND** SUCCESSFULLY REIGNED DURING FORTY-SEVEN YEARS.   HE DIED IN THE SEVENTY-THIRD **YEAR OF** HIS AGE,

JAN\. XXVIII., ANNO DOMINI DCCCXIIII.

INDITION **VII.**

crated by Pope **Leo** III.   Three hundred and sixty-five prelates assisted at the ceremony.   Though pillaged by the Northmen in 881, and restored by Otto III. in 983, it is still in all essential respects the church of Karl.   The railings of the eight arcades of the triforium, cast in bronze, of four different patterns, and the doors, adorned with lions' heads of the same material, but not now in their original position, convey a perfect idea of the state of art in the eighth century.

On the floor in the centre of the nave there is now a large slab of marble, bearing the inscription CAROLO MAGNO, beneath which once reposed the remains of Karl.   The vault **below** was opened by Otto **III.** in 997, and again **by** Frederic Barbarossa in 1165, when the body of Karl was found seated on a throne as if alive, clothed with the Imperial robes, with the crown on his head and the sceptre in his hand ; while the sword "Joyeuse" was placed by his side, and the pilgrim's pouch which he had always worn when living was suspended to his girdle.   On his knees **was a** MS. of the Gospels. His body was enshrined by order of Frederic.   The other relics, previously removed by Otto III., were carefully preserved, and used

32. Warnings of the approaching death of the King **were** very numerous, and were noticed by **the** King himself, as well as by others. For three years before his death **there** were frequent eclipses of **the** sun and moon, and black spots were noticed **on** the sun during seven successive days. **The** portico, which had been built with great labour **between** the church and palace, suddenly fell down to the very foundation on the day of the Ascension of our Lord. Also the wooden bridge over the Rhine at Mainz, on which a wondrous amount of toil and **pains had** been expended during ten years, so that **it seemed** a thoroughly durable and permanent **structure, was** accidentally burnt down in three hours. The destruction was so complete that there did **not** remain above water-mark sufficient wood for the making of a lance shaft. Again, while **the** King was in Saxony, carrying on **his last** expedition against Godofrid, King of the Danes, **one** day when

in the coronation ceremonies of succeeding Emperors ; they are now at **Vienna.** **The throne on** which the body of Karl was seated is in **the upper nave** gallery ; it is of white marble, and in shape somewhat resembles that of Edward **the** Confessor at Westminster Abbey. **The** arches of the gallery **are** adorned with thirty-two **pillars of marble,** granite, and porphyry, brought from Ravenna **and Rome.** The present choir was commenced in 1353.

This account **of the** church at Aachen is taken from Mr. Weale's book on Belgium, Aachen, and Köln, by his kind permission.

the march had already begun, the King, having left
the camp before sunrise, saw fall suddenly from
heaven, with a great light, a blazing torch passing
through the clear sky from right to left.   While
all were wondering what this might portend, the
horse on which the King was riding fell down suddenly on its head, and he was thrown to the
ground with such violence that the clasp of his
cloak was broken and his sword-belt burst.

He was ungirt by his attendants, who hastened
to his assistance, and with some difficulty lifted up
again.   The javelin which he happened to be holding in his hand at the time was thrown from his
grasp a distance of more than twenty feet.

There occurred, too, frequent shakings of the
palace at Aachen, and constant crackings of the
ceilings of the houses in which he dwelt.   The
church in which he was afterwards buried was
struck by lightning, and the golden apple which
adorned the summit of the roof was displaced and
thrown on to the adjoining house of the priest.
There was in the same church, on the ring of the
cornice, which ran round the interior of the building
between the upper and lower arches, an inscription
in red letters, which related who was the founder
of the church ; the last line ended with the words

KAROLUS PRINCEPS.   It was noticed by some
people that in the year in which he died, and a few
months before his death, the letters which formed
the words PRINCEPS were so faded as scarcely to
appear at all.   The King either pretended not to
notice all these warnings from on high, or he
despised them and treated them as if they in no
way related to himself.[1]

33. Karl determined to make a will, in order
that he might make some **provision** for his
daughters and illegitimate children ; but he was very
dilatory in beginning it, and it was never completed.
Three years, however, before his death, he made
a division of his treasures, money, garments, and
other chattels in the presence of his friends and
attendants, making· them witnesses, that after his
death his wishes might take effect and be ratified
by their assent.   What he wished to be done with
each portion he set down in an abstract, of which
the following is a list and description :—

In the name of the omnipotent Lord God, Father,
Son, and Holy Ghost.

Description and division—made by the most
illustrious and most pious prince, Karl, Emperor,

---

[1] This was a very superstitious age.

Augustus, in the year of the incarnation of our
Lord Jesus Christ 811, in the year of his reign in
Frankia 43, in Italy 37, and of the Imperial dignity
11, and Indition 4, which holy motives and fore-
thought determined him to set about, and which by
God's will he effected—of the valuables and moneys
which were found in his treasury on that day. By
this means he was most anxious to provide that
both the customary distribution of alms which is
always made by Christians from their possessions
should be given by himself from his goods in due
order and proportion, and also that his heirs, having
all cause of doubt removed as to what ought to
belong to each of them, might be able to make
the division in proper shares, without any strife
or contention. With this object and intention he
decreed that all his goods and chattels, whether of
gold, or silver, or precious stones, or regal orna-
ments, which should be found in his treasury on that
day, as has been before said, should be divided into
three portions. These portions were then to be
again divided, two of them into twenty-one parts ;
the other portion he reserved entire. The reason
of this division of two-thirds of his property into
twenty-one parts was because that was the recog-
nized number of the metropolitan cities of his

realm. **One** of these twenty-one parts was to **be** given **by his heirs** and friends **to each** metropolis, **as** a gift of alms ; and the Archbishop who should **at** that time be the head of that church, as soon as he **had** received the gift, **was** to divide it with **his** suffragans in these proportions—one-third was to be retained for his **own** church, and **the** remaining two-thirds were **to be** divided among the suffragans.

These portions of the first threefold **division,** twenty-one in number, that **being** the number **of** the metropolitan cities, were separated from **one** another, and each stored distinct **in** its own depository, with the name of the place upon it to **which it** was to be conveyed. The names of the **metropolitan** cities to which this **grant** of alms or bounty **was to** be made were—Rome, **Ravenna,** Milan, Friuli, Gratz, **Köln,** Mainz ; Juvavum, also called Salzburg ; Trier, Sens, Besançon, Lyons, Rouen, Rheims, Arles, Vienne, Moutiers **in** the Tarantaise, Embrun, Bordeaux, Tours, Bourges. The one-third portion which **he** wished to **be** reserved intact was **to be** thus disposed of, the other two portions being assigned according to the above division and secured under his seal—this third portion was to be used for daily requirements, as **property** which had not passed **by** disposal from

the power of the possessor, and was so to remain
as long as he lived or as long as he thought its
possession necessary to him. But after his death or
voluntary abdication of worldly estate, it was to be
divided into four portions. Of these, the first was
to be added to the aforementioned twenty-one
portions; the second was to be apportioned to his
sons and daughters and their children, being
divided among them in just and reasonable proportions; the third was to be applied to the poor,
in accordance with Christian custom; and the
fourth likewise, as a gift of alms, was to come to,
and be distributed among, the men-servants and
maid-servants who formed the household of the
palace.

He also willed that there should be added to this
one-third portion of the whole, which like the other
portions consisted of gold and silver, all the vessels
and utensils which were in use in the various
departments of the household, whether of brass or
iron or other metal, together with all the arms,
clothing, and whatever else, costly or common, such
as hangings, coverlets, tapestries, hair cloths,
leather work, cushions, which should be found in
his chests or wardrobes on that day, so that by this
addition more numerous divisions might be made

of this portion, and a greater number share in this distribution of alms.

He gave directions that his chapel, under which was included all such things as pertained to the service of the Church, should be kept entire, both those things which he himself had made or collected, and those also which he had inherited from his father ; and they were in no way to be divided. But if there should be found anywhere vessels, or books, or other furniture, which should clearly appear were not given by him to the chapel, any one who wished to possess them might buy them at a just valuation and keep them for himself. He likewise declared concerning his books, of which he had made a large collection in a library, that those persons who wished to have any of them, might buy them at a fair price and the money be distributed among the poor.

Among other treasures and valuables, there were three silver tables and one gold one, of very singular size and weight. Concerning these, he willed and declared that one of the silver tables, a square one, having on it a plan[1] of the city of Constantinople, should be carried to Rome, with other appointed gifts, to the church of the blessed

----

[1] " Descriptio."

Peter, the Apostle; that the second, a round one, on which is a representation [1] of the city of Rome, should be taken to the episcopal church of Ravenna; and that the third, which far surpassed the others in the beauty of its workmanship and the heaviness of its weight, and which, being made of three connected plates, set forth a plan [2] of the whole world in a very clever and accurate configuration—this, together with the gold table which has been mentioned as the fourth, he appointed to be for the increase of the portion which was to be divided among his heirs and in alms.

He made and decreed this disposition and settlement before those Bishops, Abbots, and Counts, who were able to be present at the time. The following is a list of their names :—

Bishops : Hildebald,[3] Rikolf,[4] Arno,[5] **Wolfar,**[6] Bernoin,[7] Laidrad,[8] John,[9] Theodulf,[10] Jesse,[11] Heito,[12] Waltgaud.[13]

Abbots : Frederick,[14] Adalung,[15] Engelbert,[16] **Irmin.**[17]

---

[1] "Effigies." [2] "Descriptio." [3] Köln. [4] Mainz.
[5] Salzburg. [6] Rheims. [7] Besançon. [8] Lyons. [9] Arles.
[10] Orleans. [11] Amiens. [12] Basel. [13] Lüttich.
[14] Abbot of S. Bertin, at S. Omer.
[15] Abbot of S. Vedast, at Arras.
[16] Abbot of S. Ricquier, at Abbeville.
[17] Abbot of S. Germain, at Paris.

Counts : Walacho, Meginher, Otulf, Stephen, Unruoch, Burchard, Meginhard, Hatto, Rihwin, Edo, Ercangar, Gerold, Bero, Hildiger, Rocculf.

His son Ludwig, who by divine will succeeded him, having examined this same summary, carried out all these instructions with the greatest fidelity as soon as possible after the death of the King.

END OF EGINHARD'S HISTORY.

CHAPTER V.

FIRST great division : Among the sons of Ludwig the Pious, by the Treaty of Verdun, 843 :—

(1.) The Eastern or pure German Kingdom, of which Ludwig was King.

(2.) The Western or Neustrian Kingdom, of which Karl the Bald was King, and which was called after him Karolingia ; the capital Laon.

(3.) The Central Kingdom, a long narrow strip between the two former, extending from sea to sea, from Holland to Provence, of which Lothar was King, and which was called after him Lotharingia. Lothar became Emperor, and ruled the subject Kingdom of Italy.

Almost all the Empire was again united under the Emperor Karl the Fat, on whose deposition, in 887, there occurred the second great division, into

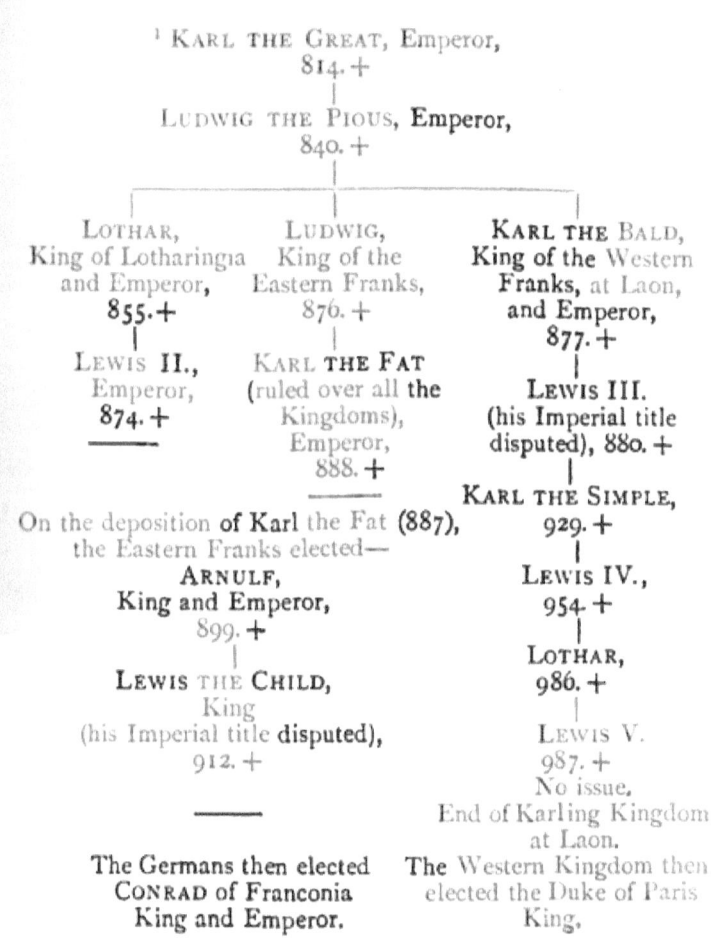

¹ KARL THE GREAT, Emperor,
814. †

LUDWIG THE PIOUS, Emperor,
840. †

LOTHAR, King of Lotharingia and Emperor, 855. †	LUDWIG, King of the Eastern Franks, 876. †	KARL THE BALD, King of the Western Franks, at Laon, and Emperor, 877. †
LEWIS II., Emperor, 874. †	KARL THE FAT (ruled over all the Kingdoms), Emperor, 888. †	LEWIS III. (his Imperial title disputed), 880. †
		KARL THE SIMPLE, 929. †
On the deposition of Karl the Fat (887), the Eastern Franks elected— ARNULF, King and Emperor, 899. †		LEWIS IV., 954. †
LEWIS THE CHILD, King (his Imperial title disputed), 912. †		LOTHAR, 986. †
		LEWIS V. 987. † No issue. End of Karling Kingdom at Laon.
The Germans then elected CONRAD of Franconia King and Emperor.		The Western Kingdom then elected the Duke of Paris King.

four kingdoms :

(1.) **The German** Kingdom, which **elected Arnulf as its** King.

(2.) The Western Kingdom, at Laon, ruled over by Karlings until 987, when **the** Duke of Paris was chosen King ; from that time the Kingdom of France.

(3.) The **Kingdom of Italy, for** a time in great disturbance, **and then** again the subject Kingdom of the German Emperors.

(4.) Burgundy, two Kingdoms, afterwards united, formed out of **the southern** portion of Lotharingia—one **by Boso in** 879, which comprised Provence, Dauphiné, part of Savoy, **and the country** between the Saone and Mount Jura ; **the** other by **Rudolf in** 888, **which** took in **the** other **portion** of Savoy **and** north-west **of** Switzerland. These **were** united under **the name of** the Kingdom **of** Arles in 937, and passed to the Empire on the death **of** the last independent King, in 1032.[1]

---

[1] Concerning the different Kingdoms of Burgundy, see Mr. Bryce's " Holy Roman Empire," Appendix A.

LONDON : PRINTED BY WILLIAM **CLOWES** AND SONS, STAMFORD STREET AND **CHARING** CROSS.